# TRADWIFE

## T C PARKER

*For my daughter, and my son*

*May you both grow up unencumbered by "traditional values"*

# CONTENT WARNINGS

Perhaps unavoidably, given the topics it explores, this book contains:
Gendered violence and misogyny
Sexual assault
Domestic abuse
Coercive behaviour
Murder and mutilation of bodies
Drug use and addiction (off-page)

8 MARCH 2024, 9.46AM

**To**: helen.kressler@nextwavepress.co.uk

**From**: jagruti.gohil@harps.ac.uk

**Re:** Gina

Hi Helen,

I'm so sorry to contact you out of the blue, especially since we haven't properly met, but I wasn't sure who else I should speak to about this, and since so many of the notes in the attached were *addressed* to you, I thought you might be the right person to speak to in the first instance. Or *one* of the right people? I'm still debating whether I should've taken it straight to the police instead.

Anyway.

We haven't met, as I say, but I expect you'll have twigged already from the email address who I am – that I'm Gina Lewis' wife. Or... I *hope* I still am. The last couple of weeks have left me quite disorientated. About everything.

I expect you also know already what's been going on at our end. I told the officers I spoke to when I filed the missing person's report that you'd been working with Gina on a project, and they said they'd be speaking to you in due course, so I assume they've got to that by now.

Suffice to say, nothing's changed in the fortnight since I called them and filed that bloody report: Gina's still gone, nobody's been able to trace her, and honestly, I'm losing my mind trying to work out what the hell might have happened to her. I daresay most of the people who know about her disappearing think she's just up and left me, and that I'm in denial. But you *know* Gina: you know what she's like, how she operates. She's a talker. If she was going to leave me, she'd sit me down and guide me through a bullet-point laundry list of all the things that were wrong with our relationship and all the reasons it couldn't be salvaged. She wouldn't sneak out in the middle of the night without saying a word.

And she definitely wouldn't have left her phone behind. Or her laptop.

I've been tearing the house apart looking for some sort of clue about where she might've gone – what might have happened to her. We've always respected each other's privacy, so I held off on logging into the computer longer than I should have, but after a while the worry became more pressing than my ethics.

(Probably not much to offer in mitigation, but I didn't actually break into the bloody thing: she keeps her passwords on a set of Post-it notes around the office. That's Gina all over, isn't it? Open, trusting. Too open and trusting for her own good, sometimes).

A lot of the recently opened documents relate to the project she's been working on for you and Next Wave – the

Tradwife book. And the *most* recent is the one I'm sending on here, footnotes and all, which reads to me like a nearly finished first draft. There's also an audio file –a recording of an interview it looks like she hadn't got around to typing up. I'm attaching that too... though if I'm right about the order, it makes more sense to listen to it *after* you've read the document.

She told me she's been keeping her cards close to her chest about the contents, and that you've given her free editorial rein to pursue whatever avenues she likes, as long as she meets her deadline. I'm assuming you haven't read or listened to much – or any – of it already. But I'm sharing it now in the hope you *will* read it, even in its unfinished form, and that you'll consider contacting me when you have, so we can talk through your impressions of it. I'd be so, so grateful if you would.

I'm not saying it's definitely the key to anything, or that there are, I don't know... hidden coordinates buried in the text that'll tell us where she is or how to find her. Probably I'm seeing things that aren't there because I *want* to see them. Because I *want* there to be some explanation for all of this that isn't my wife's body lying in the Thames some-where, waiting to wash up on a riverbank.

Some of the things she's written, some of the things she seems to have found out in the course of researching the Tradwife book, and the way she reacts to what she hears in that last interview... they raise questions, for me. As does the fact the whole thing ends on such an abrupt note, right after that interview – that's got to mean some-thing, surely?

I'm aware even as I write this that I'm rambling and oversharing and contradicting myself, and I know this is a lot, coming from someone you've never met who's slid into your inbox. I'm just... I'm at a loss. I need to know what the hell is going on. I need to know how to fix it.

And I need Gina back. If there's even the remotest chance that you reading the book and listening to the file and seeing something in it all will help me do that, then it doesn't matter how much of a lunatic I seem, does it?

Please, please: read the attachment, then play the audio, as soon as you can. And call me once you have. My mobile and office number are in the signature below.

Once again – I'm so sorry for the intrusion, for throwing all this at you so abruptly. I wish so badly I didn't have to.

Jags

# TRADWIFE: MURDER AT THE HEART OF SOLOMON[1]

## By

## GINA LEWIS

## Word Count: TBC

---

[1]. Helen – is this title okay? Too sensationalist? Not sensationalist enough? I want to make sure we clarify early on that this isn't just another exploitative true crime rehash - but I also don't want us to end up with something so dry and academic-sounding that people switch off before they've even read the blurb.

Let me know what you think – G.

# INTRODUCTION

On the 21st of September 2019, two married couples – Jason and Aisling Wilson, and Brendan and Rebecca Cooper – attended a dinner party at the home of a third couple, Freddie and Nadine Taylor.

Sometime between 8pm that evening, when Nadine called her twin eight-year-old sons at their grandmother's house to wish them goodnight, and 7.30am the following morning, when the Taylors' gardener Dev Thakar entered his employers' kitchen and encountered the bloodbath inside, all six were murdered.

No bodies – no full, *intact* bodies – were found at the house. A number of body *parts*, however, were found in and around the kitchen and dining room, which subsequent DNA sampling confirmed as belonging to the Taylors, the Coopers and the Wilsons.

Much has already been written about the details of Mr Thakar's discovery and the police investigation that followed, often in forensic detail, and I have little to add to what's been documented. It is however, and with apologies to those readers who may find such detail difficult to stomach, incumbent on me to give a brief inventory of the body parts left behind, if only to more accurately set the scene.

Under the dining table, in a pool of their own congealed blood, lay a portion of the severed tongue of Aisling Wilson and the raggedly removed left hand of her husband, the latter still wearing its rose gold wedding band. A surgical-grade scalpel had been used to extract Aisling's tongue; Jason's hand, meanwhile, had been separated from the wrist with a meat cleaver or similarly sharp butcher's implement.[1]

Forensic pathologists later determined that the same sharp blade had been used to amputate Rebecca Cooper's feet, both of which Mr Thakar found placed by the back door beside a pile of the Taylors' outdoor shoes: a particularly grisly visual gag on the killer's part. Brendan Cooper's penis and testicles, conversely, had been removed with a duller blade, most likely a bread knife, and deposited in the food bowl of the Taylors' Alaskan Malamute, Augustus – also missing since the time of the murders.

An assortment of teeth, identified through dental records as Nadine Taylor's, had been scattered like dice across the dining room carpet, along with her fingernails, a section of her scalp and a substantial portion of her white-blonde hair.

Most shockingly from Mr Thakar's perspective, however – as he himself has since related in interview – was the dining table's centrepiece[2]: Freddie Taylor's heart, presented on a stoneware platter on top of a bed of salad

---

1. Helen – do we need to include the post-mortem reports here? I'm trying to keep the actual description brief but can add them in, or link to them, if you think they'll add credibility.
2. Hyland, G. (2019) '"The Worst Thing I've Ever Seen In My Life": Gardener Who Discovered Heart of Solomon Bloodbath Speaks Out.' *Daily Express*, 15 October, p1.

leaves. The heart and its valves had been sliced carefully into quarters; the rather mangled appearance of one of these quarters, and specifically the markings in the tissue he identified at the time as bite marks, gave Mr Thakar the impression that a part of the heart had already been eaten.[3]

The downstairs of the house was awash with blood, subsequently established through DNA testing as originating from all six victims – though none, curiously, had been left by the vanished dog. This, in combination with the excised body parts, proved sufficient evidence for Nottinghamshire police – the force who initially took charge of the investigation – to label the mutilation and disappearance of the Wilsons, the Taylors and the Coopers not as a missing persons case, but as murder. Freddie's fourth-generation Range Rover, taken from the Taylor garage on the night of the killings but never found, is widely believed to have been used to transport the bodies from the property and out of the wider Heart of Solomon site.

The marked and decidedly inconvenient absence of footage from, for example, CCTV and video-doorbell cameras – both of which were strictly forbidden across the Heart of Solomon site, where the privacy of residents was deemed of significant importance to override any security concerns – only complicated the investigative proceedings that followed.

Almost four years on, no perpetrators have been identified. No charges have been laid, and despite intense and enduring international media interest, the case remains unsolved.[4]

---

3.  Ibid.
4.  Too melodramatic? I could almost hear the *Law & Order* theme tune playing in my head as I was writing it...

One need not be a Freudian to infer that the specific nature of the mutilations was likely intended to relay a message: to communicate some symbolic meaning to the police, and possibly even the general public. Nor, given what is now widely known of the victims, is it difficult to imagine why each victim was maimed as they were: why Brendan Cooper, for example, was castrated, or why Nadine Taylor – as well-known for the dazzling brightness of her smile, the ironed perfection of her hairstyle and the fire engine red of her manicured fingernails as for her politics – was left scalped, de-nailed and toothless.

The context of these particular crimes, though – the backdrop against which they were committed – imbues them with a greater symbolic significance still. It's also, arguably, the reason the British public remain so fascinated with the case, so long after it occurred.

Because the Wilson, Taylor and Cooper murders took place not in a conventional suburban neighbourhood, as the dinner party setting might suggest, but in the Heart of Solomon: Britain's first, and, so far, *only* dedicated Tradwife community.

———

There's much to say, and much that *has been* said about the doctrines and philosophies of the Tradwife movement, in the UK, US and elsewhere – some of which we'll touch on in the chapters that follow.

But for now, we can perhaps restrict ourselves to broad-stroke summaries and definitions.

While the origins of the neologistic term "Tradwife" are murky, global search engine data points to a groundswell of cultural interest in the phenomenon at the tail-end of the

2010s, which continued into the 2020s. A portmanteau of "traditional" and "wife," "Tradwife" denotes a contemporary female homemaker with traditionalist (usually conservative) views on the nature of gender roles within and beyond the bounds of heterosexual marriage and the nuclear family. Tradwives, the most generous definitions tell us, are simply stay-at-home wives and mothers: women who, with the financial support of their husbands, choose to perform everyday labour in the domestic sphere and not the workplace.

In practice, British and American Tradwives – if the hundreds of thousands of images and videos corresponding to the #tradwife hashtag and its various permutations across social media platforms are any indication – are almost uniformly white, cisgender and of a slimmer body type than current UK and US averages.[5] They are often, or appear to be, middle-class; middle-class enough, at least, that they're financially able to eschew paid work while supported only by their partners' salaries. Like the archetypal 1950s housewife, their ideological forbear, they cook, clean, mend and stitch; tend to their homes and husbands, and lavish attention on their own physical appearance, the better to maintain the sexual interest *of* those husbands.

They take, of course, great pride in doing so.

Many, though not all, also subscribe to a set of quasi-political and religious beliefs more commonly associated with 1950s Christian America than the pluralism of the present-day UK. "Tradwife marriages" are often *Biblical* marriages: fundamentally patriarchal, predicated on the submission of the wife to her husband and his will.

---

5.  That they're heterosexual, or at the very least in heteronormative relationships, feels like a given. Is it even worth mentioning?

Researchers and journalists like Fran Ashburn have explicitly connected the growth of Tradwives, and of the less hashtag-friendly but perhaps more established "traditional marriage" movement, with the rise of the North American and European far-right and its attendant beliefs: in Christian nationalism, white supremacism, rigid male/female sex and gender norms, and the primacy of monogamous male/female pairings. The very concept of the Tradwife, some have argued, represents one strand of a US (and to a lesser extent, UK) conservative backlash against "progressive" values, and the kind of technological innovation once framed as having "freed" women from the kitchen in the mid-20th century: evidence of a nostalgia on the part of some conservative women for an imagined era of slow-paced living, low divorce rates, and home-cooked meals prepared from scratch. An era uncomplicated by any considerations of structural inequality, ecological meltdown or economic precarity.

The Tradwife movement, like so many conservative creeds and enterprises, is driven, or so it seems to me, by fear: fear of change, fear of the unfamiliar and the Other, and fear of an uncertain future that may look and feel very different than today.[6]

And it was on these very fears that Freddie and Nadine Taylor capitalised, in creating the Heart of Solomon.

———

At the time of the murders, the Heart of Solomon micro-community housed twelve married couples and their chil-

---

6. Feels a bit polemical and soapbox-y... but then, are we even trying for objectivity, really?

A winding strip of oak framed cottages constructed on a disused parcel of agricultural land in South Nottinghamshire, the Heart of Solomon was envisaged by the Taylors as a sort of purpose-built Stepford: a semi-rural but well-connected idyll not far from the A6, in which "traditional" families could live out their Pleasantville fantasies in the company of men and women who shared their credo, for only £900 per calendar month plus bills. And an optional annual tithe of £5000, payable directly to the Taylors.

Admittance to the community was granted at the discretion of Freddie and Nadine, who served both as landlords of the fifteen properties that comprised the Solomon site and as its de facto gatekeepers. Rental applications were invitation-only; open, as of the Taylors' deaths, exclusively to those already known to them through the predominantly online Tradwife and "traditional family" networks with which they were so heavily involved, and to whom Freddie directed much of the video and article content curated on his *Fresh Meat* and *Family Man* websites and YouTube channels.

Press releases and supporting promotional materials, disseminated by the Taylors' PR agency in the run-up to the Heart of Solomon's launch, described the community as a "Tradwife paradise on earth," and later as "the Green and Pleasant Home of TradFam Values." Elsewhere, clips shared on Nadine's *In The TradLife* channel speak more explicitly to potential Tradwife tenants: urging them to "watch this space" for news on the progress of the Heart of Solomon project, and offering tips on ways in which they might subtly "persuade" their husbands to consider relocation, if and when the Heart of Solomon site expanded.

Quite why the Taylors should have directed so much time, money and energy towards promoting a *closed* development remains a matter of speculation. Although some, like Raine Hudson of *Resist* magazine, have theorised that the Heart of Solomon might have been only the first in a series of planned Tradwife communities masterminded by the couple – and that Freddie had already begun in 2019 to solicit investment for these future communities from a number of US-based conservative backers.[7]

––––––

None of the surviving nine couples – the eighteen adults who remained at the Heart of Solomon immediately following the murders – were willing to be interviewed by the innumerable journalists, filmmakers and other media representatives who contacted them thereafter. Nor were any amenable to interview for the purposes of *this* book. I will therefore do them the courtesy of omitting their names and identifying details here. It's worth my stating only that not one of them has been accused at any point of wrong-doing in the matter of the Taylor, Wilson and Cooper killings – but that all have likely experienced some degree of trauma as a result of their proximity to the incident, their relationships with the victims and the public scrutiny they bore thereafter, and that I have no intention of adding to that trauma by rehashing their stories and biographies here.

Others, however, *have* consented to share with me their stories of the Coopers, the Wilsons, the Taylors and the Heart of Solomon development. These subjects – the friends, families, co-workers, acquaintances and former

––––––

7. Hudson, R. (2021) 'Clean Dishes, Dirty Money: Who's Really Funding 'Traditional' Marriage?' *Resist Magazine*, 7. www.thisisresist-magazine.com

partners of the murdered victims – have been generous with their time and unflinching in their accounts, and I am supremely grateful for the kindness they extended me, in some cases despite the burden of their own grief. Many of them have never spoken of their experiences on the record before now; many, in fact, agreed to speak to *me* only after lengthy preliminary discussions of my motivations for writing this book, and how I hoped it would differ from earlier and more sensationalist accounts of the Solomon tragedy.

Their testimonies form the narrative bedrock of the chapters that follow, none of which would exist were it not for their cooperation.

———

You may be asking yourself: why am I writing this? What's my interest in the Heart of Solomon, and what fresh angle could I possibly bring to what is, by 24-hour news-cycle standards, a relatively cold case?

You might even be wondering – much as my wife did, when I first told her I'd be starting this project – why I think I, a fiction writer with neither prior involvement in nor insider knowledge of the case to bring to the table, could possibly add anything of value to a story that's already been the focus of so many Reddit forums, true crime podcasts and Netflix documentaries.

Perfectly valid concerns, all.

Before I answer, I want to emphasise that this book is absolutely *not* an attempt on my part to figure out *whodunnit*: to solve the murders that have left the police and amateur detectives the world over scratching their heads. I'm *not* a detective, of any variety; my understanding of the specifics of crime-solving is largely limited to whatever I've managed to glean from forty-plus years of devouring cosy mysteries.

I am, however – or I *was*, before the publication of *The Eight Half-Lives of Cleo McAllister* and my subsequent side-step into semi-professional confabulation – a sociologist. I've always been less interested in the complexities of the individual's psychology than in the cultural conditions that give rise to social group behaviours. TL; DR, as my wife forbids me from saying out loud in company: I care more about what people do together, and why they do it, than about what might or might not be going on in their heads.

And I found myself very interested indeed recently in the *what* and *why* of the Heart of Solomon.

I have, as per the above, no personal investment in the case, and no previous connection with any key player therein, living or dead. But the more I've read of the murders and the circumstances that precipitated them, and the more I've learned of the Taylors, the Heart of Solomon and the Tradwife movement as a whole... the more I've found myself wanting to understand how *any* of it could have happened.

How, for example, could a Trad lifestyle so very synonymous with a white American conservatism and a 1950s American Dream take root in the UK Midlands, given its very different social, religious and political history (not to say demographic composition)?

What particular set of cultural conditions allowed the Taylors' vision to flourish as it did in that time and place, even briefly?

Most pressingly, from my perspective: regardless of who actually killed the Wilsons, the Taylors and the Coopers four years ago... to what extent was violence the inevitable final destination of a community ideology constructed on a foundation of gender-based submission and inequity?

Should we even be surprised that the Taylors' "Green and Pleasant" neighbourhood wound up soaked with blood?

Answering these questions, for me – *trying* to answer them, at any rate – means getting to know the Heart of Solomon and its residents, retrospectively: building profiles of the victims, their relationships and the worldview they shared, through conversations with those who knew them best. It means unpicking the Taylors' business practices and following the money that transformed a plot of derelict farmland into a reactionary utopia. It means examining what spurred ostensibly ordinary people like the Coopers and the Wilsons to join what could easily look, to the uninitiated, like a misogynist cult.

More than anything, it means asking: what is it that *makes* a Tradwife? What does she believe?

And what kind of a society, or even a microcosm of a society, allows beliefs like hers to flourish?

## WHY ME? - A PERSONAL NOTE

*N.B. Helen – I'm not sure at all about including this section in the final draft. I appreciate the need to bring a bit of my own personality to the copy – to "give it an emotional core," I think was how you put it? But this might be... a bit much. I don't know if I'd tell my therapist some of this stuff, if I had one.*

*Anyway... see what you think – G.*

I first read about the Heart of Solomon murders on my wedding day.

Neither of us wanted a fuss, and to this end we'd kept things very deliberately small-scale: just us, two witnesses my now-wife knew from her running club (chosen, equally deliberately, because they were acquaintances, not friends) and the registrar attached to Lambeth Town Hall.

It was a lovely ceremony, both affirming and exactly as brief as we'd hoped it would be. Afterwards, we took the Tube home, in our suits and boutonnières, and I happened to pick up a copy of the Metro someone had left behind on the seat next to me.

And saw the headline: Six Slain In Midlands Tradwife Cult.

The accompanying story, which of course I read, cast something of a pall over the remainder of the day: not because of the horror of the incident itself, per se, but because of the things in my own life I was reminded of. The memories stirred.

It's true, as I mentioned earlier in this Introduction, that I have no personal stake in the Heart of Solomon case or its resolution; that those involved are strangers to me.

It's also true, however, that my own personal history makes me perhaps... more predisposed than others to take an interest in the Solomon story.

Here's the thing (with apologies for the slightly Dickensian tenor of the text hereafter):

Like Freddie Taylor, I was born in 1979, in my case to a teenage mother and a "father" who vanished from the scene not long after my conception. My actual birth took place in the attic bedroom of a Georgian terrace house in Ladbroke Grove —which belonged, at the time, to a man named Johnny Mahoney. Or rather, as he styled himself then, the Reverend John Lovemore: founder and leader-in-perpetuity of the Free People's Collective.

A low-rent London answer to Jim Jones' Peoples Temple, and the many similar cults that proliferated across the US in the 1970s, the FPC was also, at heart, a testament to female servitude and male supremacy. Comprising Mahoney himself, a small, handpicked group of his lieutenants (all of them men), and a revolving door of young, white and vulnerable teen and twentysomething girls (typically 15-20 of them at any one time), all of whom lived together at the Ladbroke Grove house, the FPC preached a familiar, toxic gospel: of "free love," faith healing, non-specific "enlightenment" (chiefly achievable through opiate and hallucinogen consumption), and conspiracy-laden suspicion of UK government authorities.

In practice, this equated to all the things we've come to expect of '70s misogynist cults. Unlimited and unfettered sexual access to acquiescent female bodies for a select few men – and rape an occurrence so commonplace it came to be normalised for the girls in question. A blanket ban on allopathic medical treatment for acute and chronic illness, regardless of need - culminating in unnecessary pain and suffering for all involved. Drug abuse resulting in frequent sickness and overdose; ritualistic fasting and meditative practices that kept Mahoney's supplicants in a constant state of near starvation.

And, of course, domestic labour, performed exclusively by the women of the FPC: the cooking, cleaning and household management that ensured Mahoney and his boys were "looked after" as well in Ladbroke Grove as they might once have been by their own mothers.

*My* mother had been drawn into the FPC – or so she'd tell me many years later, in one of our few conversations about that period of her life – after a chance meeting with Mahoney at Charing Cross. She was seventeen, homeless, and four months' pregnant; had been sleeping rough in a succession of Underground stations following her forcible ejection from the family home by my maternal grandfather, whom I never met, but who - my mother assured me - took violent objection to both her pregnancy and the mixed-Caribbean heritage of the man who'd impregnated her. Mahoney, resplendent in saffron salwar kameez and with a predator's eye for vulnerability, spotted her begging by the station entrance; chatted to her, bought her a cup of tea and a cream bun from a cafe across the road, and just a few minutes later, invited her to stay with him and his friends at their commune out west.

She, with few other options at her disposal, accepted the offer. And, upon entering the FPC, remained in its clutches for the six years thereafter – giving birth in that attic room, and raising me downstairs, among her FPC "family."

The memories I have of the place are as hazy as you might expect, given my age at the time. I recall playing in the kitchen with some of the girls there, girls who might have been my older sisters, while they boiled eggs and peeled vegetables and chased me around with a dustpan and brush; listening to Culture Club and the Flying Pickets on the radio (there was no television in the house) with my mother whenever Mahoney was out, because he'd forbidden his disciples from engaging with "modern technology"; sleeping on a sheet-less mattress in a room with seven or eight other people and watching their breath and the heat from their bodies steam up the windows. The house had no boiler, no central heating; not even double-glazing to keep in whatever warmth there was.

Mahoney himself was a distant figure, as disinterested in me as I was in him. Unlike some of those other cult leaders he sought to emulate – the Children of God's David Brandt Berg, for example – he expressed no love of or affection for kids; not once, that I remember, did he talk to me directly, or play with me as some of the women did, or touch me anywhere, in any way. His attention was reserved for the older girls: the ones who did his laundry, washed his feet and joined him in his bed at night.

For this, if nothing else about the experience, I'm grateful.

I don't know why my mother left Ladbroke Grove and the FPC when she did, at the start of '85. Nor do I know exactly *how* she left: my memories of *that* night extend only to raised voices and flashes of arguments half-heard through a door, mosaic-like images of clothes thrust into a suitcase and my own arms pulled roughly into a duffel coat, and a very slightly more vivid recollection of boarding a double-decker with my mother, in the dark, sour with disappointment at her refusal to let me sit alone on the top deck.

What happened to us after *that*, I know principally through acts of reconstruction: piecing together, document by document, the paper trail she left behind for me.

In late 1985, presumably after a period in which we couch-surfed – or perhaps availed ourselves of whatever women's refuge services were available to Londoners in the mid-80s – we were allocated a two-bedroom council flat in Willesden. We lived there together until I left for university aged 18, after which she lived there alone until her death, in 2011, from complications relating to early-onset Alzheimer's disease. Or, more formally, Wernicke-Korsakoff syndrome: alcohol-related dementia.

She was 49.

I'm not, I know, the only person out there with a parent who drank themselves to death, but I may be one of a smaller number of those whose parent's alcoholism can be linked directly to their experience of what was, in effect, a misogynist cult.

She rarely talked about the years she spent in the FPC, and more often than not became angry, defensive – and then passive-aggressively silent – when I raised the subject. I felt the aftershocks of those years, however, throughout the first decades of my life. Through her erratic behaviours and propensity to disappear from the flat for days at a time with no explanation, only to return with a man – always a different man – I'd never met before, and who'd stay with us for a handful of weeks before vanishing as quickly as he'd appeared; in the difficulties she encountered holding down a job, and bringing in the money we needed to keep food in the fridge and the bailiffs from the door. And, obviously, in the alcoholism itself: the taste for vodka and gin, then Diamond White and Special Brew, that harvested her hair and her teeth, her internal organs and her mind as efficiently – if with an altogether more painful slowness – as any Heart of Solomon killer.

I'm in no doubt, having spoken since her death to several survivors of the FPC – one of whom felt able to leave only after Mahoney's sudden expiration, from a heart attack, in 1994 – that the daily traumas she must have endured at the Ladbroke Grove house, and the post-traumatic stress that must have lingered after, contributed in large part to the problems she suffered in what she would often refer to, chillingly, as "the world outside." The rapes and druggings; the regular "punishment" beatings she and the other girls took from Mahoney and his foot-soldiers; the servitude; the constant, all-pervading paranoia about "state surveillance" and "bad actors" that permeated the walls of the place... any one of these abuses, over a period of years, would be enough to drive a person to self-medicate. Like so many cult members, she became institutionalised – but, lacking access to those support services that might (one hopes) now be offered to survivors, she was unable to reorient herself "outside."

And therein, perhaps, lies my real reason for writing this book. My mother is dead; long dead. There's no way for me now to understand why she made the decisions she made, all those years ago: why she stayed at the FPC as long as she did; what coping mechanisms she drew on, and how she got through the day.

I'll never know for sure what spell, what thrall Mahoney was able to cast over her. Or what finally happened to break it.

Perhaps I'm being excessively optimistic. Perhaps whatever parallels I've drawn in my head between the FPC and the Heart of Solomon are misplaced – but a part of me hopes nevertheless that, in beginning to understand Solomon, and the Taylors and the Coopers and the Wilsons of the world, I can begin to understand my mother, and what she decided for us both, back then. Even if only in the rear-view mirror.

# AUNTIE ANN

If you're only passingly familiar with the Tradwife movement, the name Annamaria Ainsworth probably doesn't mean much to you.

If, however, you're a Tradwife yourself – or a critic like Raine Hudson – then there's every chance that Ainsworth, or at least her nom-de-plume Auntie Ann, is as recognisable to you as Taylor Swift and the Kardashians.

In the closed-system universe of Trad living, Ainsworth is a superstar: offering advice, as Auntie Ann, on "traditional" homemaking skills, from bread-baking and cake decoration to dressmaking and stain-removal to the 2 million-plus followers of her Auntie Ann's Kitchen Instagram account.

That she agreed to speak with me about the movement

– and her association with Jason and Aisling Wilson – was, frankly, a bit of a surprise.[1]

"Fundamentally, it's about choice," she tells me – describing how she and so many women like her perceive Tradwife subculture. "For years – decades, actually – we've had people telling us that feminism is about empowerment, about women doing what they want to do, doing *whatever* they want to do. Well, what if what some women want to do is stay at home and look after their families? They're grown adults. Is that not a choice they're allowed to make for themselves?"

Ainsworth seems an unlikely advocate of third-wave feminist thinking, at least on the surface. 5'2 and maternal in the long-sleeved teal dress and pinafore with which regular visitors to her social channels will be well acquainted, her ash-blonde hair a respectable shoulder-length and her pale-porcelain skin enhanced by layers of cosmetics, she reminds me a little of the actor Felicity Kendal – her accent plummy, her delivery crisply no-nonsense. Though she refuses to disclose her age ("a lady doesn't"), I place her somewhere in her late sixties: old enough to have earned the right to dispense motherly, even grandmotherly advice to her legions of younger female fans.

Although, as she is quick to confirm early on in our

---

1. Helen – how necessary is it for me to mention how I stumbled across her, and who gave me her name as a lead to follow? I've put her interview upfront, to put a human face to the Tradwife thing, but the actual conversation happened quite a bit after I spoke to the ex-Solomon Wife, Lucy Murillo – or "Joanne," I suppose, if that's what we end up calling her. Lucy was very good about pointing me in AA's direction, but I promised her discretion, and I'd hate to have to renege on that, even if it *is* in the interests of transparency…

conversation, she herself is neither a mother nor a wife, "trad" or otherwise.

"It feels counterintuitive, doesn't it?" she says of the discrepancy between her personal life and the Auntie Ann brand. "Telling all these girls how to look after their husbands, when *I've* never had one. But that's the beauty of being an Auntie, you see – you're ever so slightly on the outside, looking in, so you have a better sense of perspective on things like what makes a marriage tick than the young ones whose only experience is being *in* one. Or the older ladies who might have come out bitter on the other side. And you've had more time, a whole *lifetime* in my case, to cultivate the sorts of skills and interests those young ones need to keep a house running smoothly. All the cooking and cleaning and whatnot.

"It's like I always say, when people ask: a vegetarian chef can still rustle up a fillet steak, can't he? And that Super-nanny – she's got no kids of her own, but all she does is tell parents how they ought to be bringing up theirs."

I enquire, tentatively, *why* she never married, if "traditional" marriage is something she believes in as fervently as she claims to in her videos.

"It just never happened for me, dear," she answers, unruffled – no doubt because the question has been put to her so often since she entered the limelight. "I never met... I don't want to say the *right* man, because I don't really believe in Mr Right. No man's going to come to you wrapped up in a bow like Prince Charming, is he? But the right man *for me*. The one I'd want to settle down and have my babies with. So, I've just sort of plodded along, on my own, trying to help other girls out where I can. Because it's so important, isn't it, family? *So* important. It's the bedrock of a healthy society. And women, wives and mothers, they're the heart of the family. We'd all be lost without them."

She delivers this last line with the polish and infectious enthusiasm of a career politician. There is, more generally, something of the orator about her, a side-effect perhaps of the teaching jobs she tells me she held before taking early retirement in her fifties: a move that freed her to pour more time and energy into crafts and baking, and the digital side-project that would eventually become Auntie Ann's Kitchen.

We meet, at her suggestion, in a knowingly old-fash-ioned and conspicuously out-of-the-way tea shop, close to her home in the Peak District. This, she explains, is where she comes to do her "thinking": to plan and write up the recipes, tutorials and straight-to-camera homilies around which she structures her online content. It also, I can't help but notice, shares a certain aesthetic similarity with the kitchen from which she broadcasts her bi-weekly videos; an overabundance of decorative bone china and rustic cabinets that wouldn't look at all out of place in Ainsworth's home studio.

As a relative stranger to Tradwife culture, and a lifelong lesbian feminist, I'm conscious that my exposure to and awareness of the movement has been filtered through a combination of my own biases and the largely negative media and academic coverage it's received. Within the circles I move in, personally as well as professionally, neither "trad" values nor "traditional marriage" are consid-ered particularly aspirational, let alone embraced as being "bedrocks of a healthy society."

I'm keen therefore to try to understand Tradwife culture on its own terms. To have its appeal and its unifying precepts explained to me by someone in the know: a supporter of the movement and its goals, whatever they might be. Someone who subscribes to its ideals.

And who better to explain them – to convince me of their worth, if such a thing is possible – than Auntie Ann?

"So many women would love to be able to stay at home, look after the house and mind the children, while their husbands take care of the bills and mortgage," she says, biting into a Bakewell Tart less tantalising than those she makes from scratch for her video audience. "But we tell them they can't, that they shouldn't want to. And why? Because we've convinced ourselves that men and women are the same, and they should want the same things. That women should get the same satisfaction from work as men do, the same *buzz*. But they don't, though, do they? If we're honest with ourselves. Men are competitive creatures, hunters and predators. They're built for aggression, one-upmanship... the sort of qualities you *should* have when you're in business. All that testosterone they've got sloshing around them, they can't help it. Men are *meant* to go out and work and put food on the table. But women are different. We're made for nurturing, not killing. It's cultivation and nourishment we're made for, if you want to get all anthropological about it. We're supposed to be back in the caves building the fires and feeding the young while the men go hunting mountain sheep and rhinos, the way we used to. It's in our blood."

So, you think it's biological, I ask her – the imperative for women to stay at home and nest while their husbands go out and fight in the corporate trenches?

"Of course. Don't you, deep down?"

No, I tell her, reluctant though I am to inject too much of myself into the interview. I'm a social constructionist, mostly; I don't really believe in hard-and-fast gender roles. I think we do what we've been conditioned to do, depending on where and when we are and how other people perceive us, and that a lot of gendered norms are just thinly veiled mechanisms for keeping people in their place.

I think we're all victims of a hegemonic patriarchy, in one way or another.

And I think a lot of evolutionary psychology theories about Neanderthal societies and sex roles are shaky, at best.

"You've never wanted a man to look after you?" she asks, flashing me a smile that leaves me with the impression that she's making fun of me, albeit gently.

I'm gay, I say. My wife and I look after each other.

"We should all be so lucky, dear," she says, still smiling.

I admit, I find myself confused by her response: so much of what I've seen of online Tradwife culture and its trumpeting of the heteronormative gold standard has come accompanied by a degree of homophobia, sometimes tacit and sometimes explicit. I arrived at our meeting expecting to encounter disapproval, should any discussion of my own sexuality or domestic circumstances arise. But Ainsworth seems only mildly amused.

Keen to stop our conversation veering any further off track, I ask her: what makes her think, as she said, that a *lot* of women want to live more "traditionally"? To keep house and "nurture" their husbands?

"They tell me!" she says, with a peal of that Felicity Kendal-esque laughter. "You should see some of the messages I get, read the comments under some of my videos. Thousands, *thousands* and thousands of women, all of them saying how much they hate going out to work and wish they could stay in, baking cakes and ironing all day. There's an epidemic of frustrated homemakers out there, all desperate to win the lottery or for their husbands to get promoted so they can make the choice to stay at home."

And there's that word again: *choice.*

Could it not just be, I suggest, that *everyone's* a bit burned out by late-stage capitalism, women *and* men,[2] and that the fantasy of Tradwife living and "traditional marriage" has been sold to a generation of tired women specifically as a way of escaping the grind?

"Well, yes," she agrees – again, to my surprise. "And why is *that?* Could it be because we've herded so many women into the workforce and told an entire generation of girls *and* boys that work is going to set them free, when all it's done is exhaust them? I worked all my life, and I tell you, nothing I ever did then gave me the sort of satisfaction I get from what I do now."

This seems as good an opportunity as any to segue into another of the questions I've been hoping to put to her.

But, I say, you still *do* work, don't you? I was under the impression you took on some consultancy jobs, here and there.

She puts down her Bakewell Tart and fixes me with a stare that, I'm not ashamed to admit, I find more than a little intimidating.[3]

"You've done your research, I see," she says, a chillier note entering that lilting champagne-flute voice. "Yes,

---

2. Conscious that I'm only mentioning categories of male and female here, and omitting non-binary people, other gender identities and so on. No excuse but my own cowardice, really: I was afraid that if she thought I was some sort of gender abolitionist, she'd up and leave and we'd lose the interview. Awkward enough I had to come out to her...

3. Probably not one to put in the final draft, but I've got to say, there's a touch of Atwood's Aunt Lydia about Auntie Ann when she's rattled. You wouldn't want to be the newlywed who smashes a dish in *that* kitchen.

though. Yes, I do the odd bit of consulting. Though I'm not sure I'd call it *work*, exactly."

What *would* you call it, I press her, if not work? What does her *consulting* entail?

"Oh, this and that. The girls who message me, who send me emails... sometimes they're after more hands-on help than I can give them in a video. It's the cooking, usually – some of them aren't used to cooking for themselves, let alone other people, and they were never taught *how* to cook growing up, so it can come as a shock when they find them-selves on their own with a dozen eggs and a mixing bowl and no-one telling them what to do with it all, even if they love the *idea* of whipping up a Black Forest Gateau or a brisket. They need a guiding hand – someone to show them the things their own mothers *ought* to have done, but never did. So, sometimes they ask me to step in, and sometimes I say yes, and I go and spend a few days with them at home, teaching them the basics. With the permission of the husbands, of course."

And yes, she confirms – they *do* pay her for the service, travel and accommodation costs and all.

"That's not why I do it, of course. I won't brag, it's not seemly, though I expect you know from all that digging you've been doing that I do alright for myself, financially. But money isn't the incentive. It's the being useful. Being able to help girls live the lives they've chosen, the best way they can."

I hesitate before embarking on my next line of ques-tioning – concerned that, prickly as she's become, I may well be about to alienate her further.

"Aisling Wilson," I venture, gripping my coffee cup. "She was one of the girls you helped?"

The already-low temperature across our table plummets further into the minuses.

"That's why you're here, then, is it?" she says, her accent temporarily slipping out of the Home Counties and into what sounds to me like the remnants of a long-abandoned Yorkshire Tyke. "You're not interested in the videos or the homemaking or any of that. You want to know about the murders. The Heart of Solomon business."

I'm interested in both, I insist.

"I don't believe that for a second. Though I suppose it makes no odds to me, you sniffing about like all those other *journalists* who pretend to want to talk to me. I've told the police everything I knew, and there wasn't much of it to tell *then*. Did I know that poor girl? Yes – and her husband, for that matter. But there's a world of difference between spending a long weekend teaching someone how to ice a sponge and knowing them well enough to say why some animal would want to kill her."[4]

There have been rumours about Jason, Aisling's husband, I say. Suggestions that he might have been violent towards her, abusive. Did you see anything like that, in the time you spent with them? Or hear anything to that effect from Aisling when the two of you were alone together?

Below her impeccable makeup, Ainsworth's jaw tightens. For a moment it seems as if she's formulating an answer.

---

4. Not to keep belabouring the point, but I *really* think we should leave Lucy's – "Joanna's," whatever – name out of this when we go to print. She was the one who told me about AA going to stay with the Wilsons, and given AA's reaction to me knowing they hired her, I don't think it would be at all wise to make that known, do you? Bad enough she might set the lawyers after us/Third Wave, but I wouldn't want her going after Lucy too – G

But no. Instead, without another word, she walks away from our table and out of the cafe, bringing our interview to an end.

# THE HEART OF SOLOMON

The cluster of houses briefly known as the Heart of Solomon sits adjacent to a tract of Nottinghamshire farmland given over to wheat and barley fields: waist-high green-gold plaits that, from a distance, partially obscure the derelict properties beyond.

Since 2021, both the fields and the houses have belonged to farmer Neil Childs – who, he tells me, snapped them up at a bargain-basement price when they went to auction in October of that year.

Mr Childs has asked that the details of our conversations be omitted from this book. He was kind enough, however, to grant me access to the former Heart of Solomon community when I visited – and to provide me with answers to a few background questions that helped to contextualise what I saw there. These answers are assimilated – unattributed, per his request – into the text below.

It will surprise no-one to learn that all fifteen of the Heart of Solomon houses have fallen to ruin since 2019, when the last surviving couple to remain on site returned their keys. Though ten of the fifteen were briefly floated on the rental market following Mr Childs' acquisition of the wider estate, there were no takers: not a single potential tenant willing to take on a residence with that kind of baggage, even at a much-reduced rate.

Truthfully, I can't blame them. Four years on from the Wilson-Taylor-Cooper murders, the Heart of Solomon estate strikes me as, for want of a better word, sinister: the twisting row of aggressively pastoral cottages surrounded by empty stretches of arable land are reminiscent of the setting of a folk horror story, even before you consider the disrepair into which the dwellings have fallen.

I elect not to venture inside the cottages once occupied by the Wilson, Taylor and Cooper families: it feels unreasonably demanding to ask permission and, even were Mr Childs to agree to let me in, I'd prefer not to be confronted by any old ghosts. Besides, I've seen the same crime scene photos as every other pundit with an interest in the case; there's not much to be gained, from my perspective, from poring over whatever pieces of Luminol-stained furniture or scraps of blood-spattered carpet the police and the SOCOs left behind.

Really, all I'm looking for from this experience is a tangible sense of place: a deeper and more visceral understanding of where — and in what circumstances — the Wilsons, the Taylors and the Coopers lived.

My initial impression, to this end, is of a low-key isolation. Even in its prime, the Heart of Solomon was a community deliberately set apart from the modern world around it: situated geographically as well as ideologically at a remove from contemporary urban and suburban life. Though the major A6 and A52 roads are readily accessible and the M1 only a short drive away, there are no amenities nearby – no supermarkets or corner shops in walking distance; no handy restaurants or bars or cafes. A car would have been required to get anywhere worth going.

I can't help but wonder how easy it would have been for the Tradwives of the Heart of Solomon, many of whom relinquished driving responsibilities to their husbands or had no driving licences themselves, to physically leave the area, if and when they ever wanted to.

And to wonder, moreover, what everyday life must have looked like for the women who made the "choice" that Annamaria Ainsworth and other "tradlife" proponents like her consider so very empowering.

# VICTIMS 1 & 2: JASON & AISLING WILSON

JASON & AISLING

Jason Wilson turned 32 only three days before his murder and dismemberment.

An early adopter of the Heart of Solomon ethos, he and his wife Aisling were among the first couples to relocate to the development: putting their mortgage-free luxury apartment on the market in February 2017, and moving soon after to a rented cottage next door to their new landlords, the Taylors.

The decision made little sense financially, especially for a man like Jason — a Sales Director on a six-figure salary whose Porsche 911 sports car and wardrobe of designer suits suggested a man more attached than most to material rewards. In terms of Jason's worldview, though, the move was a perfect fit: the logical culmination of an ultra-conservative belief system ultimately catalysed into a full-blown and violent misogyny by, among other things, his friendship with Freddie Taylor.

Those other friends of his whom I approached for interview declined to be involved with this book, as did his younger brother Andrew: a systems engineer, now living with his wife and children in Doha, Qatar. There is nothing in the publicly available profiles of Jason's early life, however (those offered by, for example, the Guardian's Graham Offily[1] and the Sunday Telegraph's Paula Deal[2]) to indicate in him a greater susceptibility to right-wing extremism than might have been found in any straight male contemporary growing up alongside him.

Born in Lincoln in September 1987 to pharmacists Des and Catherine (both deceased), Jason was by all known accounts an average and unremarkable child, neither challenging nor high achieving. "The sort you'd forget you had in the classroom," as one of his primary school teachers remembers him: quiet, unmemorable, neither popular nor notably unpopular with the other kids.[3]

His journey through secondary school seems to have passed equally uneventfully... though certain comments posted to the public Remembering The Heart of Solomon Victims Facebook group in the immediate aftermath of the murders, but since deleted, allude to the teenage Jason as a bully, prone to belittling and verbally abusing his female classmates.

On leaving Grantham's George Bower Academy aged 16 with a handful of GCSEs, Jason started an entry-level marketing job with tech developers SoftDog – a position in which he excelled, the boiler room-style atmosphere of the sales office bringing out in him a hitherto-dormant competi-


1. Offily, G. *Heads of the Household: Understanding The Men At The Heart of Solomon*. London: Kingfisher, 2020
2. Deal, P. *The Keepers of Wives: Tradhusbands & The Heart of Solomon Slaughter*. London: New Boudicca, 2020
3. Franks, T. 'Tradwife Murders: Who Was Jason Wilson?' *British True Crime Magazine*, January 2021. www.britishtruecrimemag.com

streak and a knack for persuasion that would lead him on to greater and ever more lucrative professional success.

"He was massively charismatic, when he switched it on," recalls one male SoftDog colleague, who spoke to me on condition of anonymity. "Not all the time – mostly he'd just be sitting around talking shit with the rest of the blokes. If you'd seen him then, you wouldn't have thought he was anything special. But when you got him on the phone with a potential client, or got them in the room with him, it would be like he'd suddenly developed the gift of the gab. He'd know exactly what to say, exactly what levers to pull and what buttons to press to get them to sign up to a subscription or go for a more expensive package than they'd wanted originally... they couldn't say no. It was amazing. Like magic."

Or, I decline to suggest, like a budding sociopath in action: a sociopath who was learning, as he aged, which skills he'd need to develop in the service of his own interests.

It was while Jason was still working at SoftDog, but after he'd secured a promotion which came with a transfer to the company's London office, that he first encountered Freddie Taylor: at a martial arts gym in Hoxton, no less, where both men trained for a white-collar boxing event organised by the *Hard Man Fighters* group. According to the club's records, this was sometime in January of 2014, when Jason was 26 and Freddie a few years older. Neither man completed the eight-week course of intensive training required to participate in the event; Freddie dropping out after a fortnight, and Jason two weeks after him. They did, however, become fast friends – their relationship paving the way for Jason's eventual move to the Heart of Solomon, and all that flowed from that.

Eighteen months later, in the summer of 2015, Jason met Aisling (then Aisling Driscoll) on the dating app Sparkd – a platform owned, coincidentally, by SoftDog's Singapore-based parent company LMTLSS. Within a few weeks, he and Aisling were living together in Jason's luxury apartment in Nottingham city centre; a new job, with a significant salary boost, having taken him back to the Midlands at the beginning of the year. By the *end* of that year, they were married: their wedding, at the local registry office, a small and – for Jason – uncharacteristically low-key ceremony attended only by Jason's brother Andrew, Aisling's mother Jude Driscoll and Jude's then-partner, Colin Fleetwood.

Aisling was 23 on their wedding day, and just 27 when she died. The only child of Jude and children's book illustrator Roland Gower, who emigrated to Ottawa in 1996 and had virtually no contact with his daughter thereafter, she was an intelligent and quick-witted girl who excelled academically and, according to her mother, maintained a close, supportive network of school friends throughout her early years and adolescence.

Her educational history points to Aisling as more-scholarly in inclination than her eventual husband. Attaining 4 A*s at A Level, she studied English and Philosophy at Durham University, graduating in 2013 with a first-class degree, with intentions of pursuing a career in publishing.

This plan, unfortunately, didn't come to fruition.

"There were no jobs in it," Jude Driscoll tells me, reflecting on her daughter's post-university experience of the book-world job market. "Not around here, and I got the impression they were thin on the ground even in London. And the internships, the volunteering, all the other bloody hoops you have to jump through to get a foot in the door so the big publishers will even *look at* you for a proper graduate role... *they* were in London. We talked about it, her moving down south, but it just wasn't feasible for her without a steady income, with what rents are like down there. And that's before you factor in the cost of living. I thought I might be able to help, I *wanted* to, but when we sat down and did the maths, you could see it wasn't doable. The few hundred quid a month I'd have been able to give her would've been a drop in the ocean compared to what she'd have needed to get by."

*Around here* in this instance is Loughborough: a student town on the border between Leicestershire and Nottinghamshire, at whose art college Jude lectures. It was to the family home in Thorpe Acre, Loughborough that Aisling returned after graduation – temporarily, or so she believed.

The two years that followed saw her take a succession of temporary receptionist and office administrator posts in and around the area: at a firm of insurance brokers, then a property lettings agency, a heavy equipment dealership and, finally, a chartered surveyor, none of which took her so much as a step closer to the world of publishing. This, Jude says – coupled with the perennial job insecurity of temping, and a weekly paycheque that never rose above minimum wage – caused Aisling's self-esteem to plummet.

"She was so sad all the time. *So* sad. Not like herself at all. She stopped seeing her friends, never wanted to go out. Didn't do anything much when she got back from work but lie on the sofa scrolling through her phone. That was how she met *him*, on her phone. And why he was able to get his hooks into her the way he did. Predators like him, they go after young women when they're vulnerable, don't they? Like sharks. They smell blood in the water, and start circling in."

There was, as this statement suggests, no love lost between Jude and her eventual son-in-law. Indeed, Jason – as Jude describes him – was an archetypal abusive husband: angry, possessive and controlling. She blames him entirely for the rift that developed between her and her daughter in the months that preceded the murders, during which they barely spoke.

More damningly still, she holds him responsible for Aisling's death.

# JUDE DRISCOLL

The living room of Jude Driscoll's two-bed terraced is what Warhol's Factory might have looked like, if he'd favoured feminist academia over Hollywood actors and soup cans. Multicoloured Pop Art-style portraits of female thinkers, contemporary and historical, peer out at you from every inch of wall: a screen-printed Angela Davis here, a batik Gloria Steinem there; Mary Wollstonecraft in charcoal, Isabel Allende in pen-and-ink.

"I know there's a lot of them," Jude says apologetically, as I take in the space. "I need a workshop, really, but I don't like keeping them at work, and I've never been one to let go of a piece once I've finished it."

The presence of art in the Driscoll home is unsurprising: Jude lectures in design and textiles, after all, and I already know from the brief biography on her college's website that she has a PhD in Fine Art Practice from the University of Leeds. Since obtaining it, she has exhibited work in Liverpool and Cumbria, Dublin and Dundee. The *subjects* of this work take me by surprise, though. I hadn't expected a girl like Aisling – a girl who made some of the decisions Aisling made before her death – to have emerged from quite so feminist a background.

I tell Jude as much.

"I'd call it ironic," she replies, "but it's not actually remotely funny, is it? Just another knife in the gut. And you won't believe me, *nobody* believes me, but Ash *was* a feminist. And a clever one. She'd never have thought she was less than anyone because she was a woman."

Some Tradwives say that staying at home to look after your husband *is* feminist, I tell her, remembering Annamaria Ainsworth and her Auntie Ann spiel. They say feminism is about choice, and Tradwives are just exercising their right to choose.

Jude's face clouds over – with rage, or grief, or both. "They say that, do they? Well. Do they say anything about what happens to the girls who *choose* to leave, I wonder? Because it's all very well to talk about people choosing to get *into* that life... but none of it means much if you can't choose to get out of it later, if you change your mind. *You've made your bed, so lie in it* isn't giving anyone much of a *choice*, is it?"

The fury and disgust the Tradwife movement elicits in her is palpable throughout much of our subsequent conversation. Jude Driscoll, I quickly discover, is very angry indeed, and with good reason, though a stranger might not guess as much from her clothes and demeanour. A thin, birdlike white woman in her late fifties, she looks the archetypal ageing hippy, from her purple kaftan and the streaks of pink in her otherwise grey, pixie-cut hair to the copper bangles at her wrists and the hint of marijuana smoke that lingers in the air around her. One might easily imagine her preparing herbal tinctures for the neighbours at an apothecary counter in her kitchen, or brandishing a Greenpeace banner at an anti-war march.

And yet.

"I'd kill him myself, if he weren't already out of the picture," she says of Jason, her former son-in-law. "Him and that bastard Freddie Taylor. I'd wring their necks with my own bare hands and spit on their carcasses."

There's no doubt in her mind that Jason would have deserved this fate. Were he alive now, she insists – given recent cultural conversations around domestic abuse, coupled with amendments to existing legislation around coercive control – he'd likely be in police custody, and Aisling free of his influence.

"People know more now about how men like him operate: the gaslighting, the way they isolate their victims from the people who love them. And I'm just as guilty as anyone else of not knowing much before – whatever you might think, looking at *this*." She indicates the art on the walls; the bell hooks and Judith Butler paperbacks on the shelves. "I had an inkling about him before they got married. A feeling he might not be all he seemed. But Ash was happy, and she hadn't been for so long, I was just relieved to see a bit of her old spark back, if you see what I mean? And it all happened so fast between them, the moving in together and the engagement, I'm not sure I really had time to take a step back and process it the way I should have. Though of course that's one of the ways the Jasons of the world get you, isn't it? The whirlwind courtship, the love bombing, making sure everything keeps zipping along at the speed of light so nobody has the headspace to question them or what they might be up to. It's all straight out of the abuser's playbook."

By Aisling and Jason's wedding day, however, Jude's doubts had crystallised into a deeper suspicion.

"He didn't want anyone there at the registry office. No one.[1] I don't even think he wanted me and Colin there, but we insisted. No way in hell was I missing my daughter's wedding, even if it *was* to him. But now I think he probably wanted her all to himself from the get-go – start as you mean to go on, sort of thing.

"The reception was alright, in the end. Just the four of us and his brother out for dinner at this fancy seafood restaurant in Plumtree. Though really, even that should've been a red flag: Ash couldn't stand fish, she always said it gave her a stomach-ache, and I kept wondering why she'd let him choose a place where she wouldn't be able to eat half the stuff on the menu, and on her wedding day. *Such* a red flag, now I look back on it.

"Things only *really* blew up once I found out she'd left her job, mind. Colin spotted her coming out of Tesco one afternoon, something like three o'clock on a Wednesday, and he said she looked awful, really pale and drawn, so I rang her that night to see if she was alright and if she'd been off sick... and she told me no, she wasn't working anymore, she'd handed in her notice. That Jason made enough money that she didn't need to bother worrying about a career anymore, because he could look after her and pay for everything while she stayed at home.

"And that was... well, I couldn't believe it, really. Don't

---

1. The desire for a small wedding may be the only point on which this particular bastard and I agree. Sorry again for not inviting you and Hopper (or anyone) to ours – I know Jags thinks we should have. All I can say is: the prospect of dozens of people watching us walk down the aisle brought me out in a cold sweat, and still does, even retroactively. So keeping it to just us and the Parkrun people was the best solution I could come up with that meant I'd actually be able to *get* married without vomiting down my dress shirt – G.

get me wrong: the jobs she'd *been* working were awful, they'd been sucking the life right out of her. But she'd been so absolutely intent on breaking into publishing – getting in with a small press, maybe, even if all the big ones were a closed shop. It was her end-goal, had been since she finished college. I couldn't get my head around her just... jacking everything in to be a housewife. Surely if Jason was making that much money, and he was happy enough being the breadwinner for a while, she could afford to apply to do an internship somewhere? Or she could apply to do a master's and see if she could make some decent contacts in the industry?"

Aisling did not respond well to her mother's queries and objections. Perhaps, Jude thinks now, because Jason was listening in on the call while the women were talking.

"She was furious with me. Absolutely raging. Told me she was an adult now, not a little kid, and if I didn't respect her decisions then I could fuck off out of her life and not come back. Those were the actual words she used: *fuck off out of my life*. And she and I, we'd had rows before, especially when she was a teenager, but I swear, she'd never spoken to me like that before. Not with that much venom, that much *hate*. She didn't even sound like herself when she was saying it; it was like I was talking to a completely different person than the one I knew. When she hung up on me, I couldn't even explain to Colin what had happened. I just stood there in the bedroom for half an hour with the phone in my hand, crying and shaking."

Aisling and Jude didn't speak for several months after that phone call: Aisling initially refusing to respond to her mother's texts or answer when Jude rang, and eventually sending Jude a lengthy text telling her mother, in no uncertain terms, to stay away.

Jude still has the text message, which runs to at least ten paragraphs and is littered with angry expletives and excoriating references to Jude's failings as a parent. And, though she's asked me not to reproduce it verbatim here, I can confirm the viciousness of its tone and content.

She didn't see or hear from Aisling for a further six months after receiving the text – deciding it might be best after all to give her daughter the space she'd demanded, in the hope that Aisling would eventually come around. When, finally, Aisling *did* attempt a rapprochement over the phone, Jude was so desperate to re-establish a relationship with her daughter that she was willing to sweep everything that had gone before – including her many reservations about Jason – under the carpet in pursuit of familial harmony.

"We didn't actually *see* each other, even after we'd made up," Jude says. "Not face to face. I'd text her, and she'd text back, but it was always very superficial chat. *How are you?* and *what are you up to?* – never anything much deeper than that. I'd try to ring her, but it was rare she'd pick up, and if I suggested going 'round to see her or her coming here for tea – with Jason, even – she'd fob me off. Tell me how busy she was, how much they had on, but that they'd try to pop over soon, when things calmed down a bit. It was always *we*, never *I* – she wouldn't contemplate going somewhere or doing something without him. And the *way* she texted was so... formal; that was something else I noticed. Full stops, whole sentences, no kisses on the end of messages, the way she used to use them. Half the time they read like something you'd send a colleague at work if you were trying to reschedule a meeting." Jude pauses, seeming to contemplate something. "It did strike me at one point that *he* might've been reading her texts, going through her phone. That she

was writing them as much for him to read as for me –
keeping it polite but distant, so he'd know she wasn't telling
me anything he didn't want her to."

This situation – infrequent text exchanges, deferred
meetups that never materialised – continued for several
more weeks... until Jude, exasperated, drove one evening
across to Nottingham, to Jason's flat, and asked to be let
inside.

"It was a terrible idea. I *knew* it was a terrible idea as I
was doing it. But what was I supposed to do? She was my
daughter. My only bloody daughter. I needed to see her. If
she was still upset and angry at me, I wanted to talk to her
properly and put it right. And if it was *him* – if he was
turning her against me or telling her to keep me at arm's
length – then I needed her to know I was still there, I was
still her mum and I still loved her, and I'd always *be* there
for her, whatever he said or did. I remember standing
outside that block of flats, pushing the buzzer to be let in,
and fully expecting him to come down and tell me to sod
off. I thought I'd have to argue with him there and then, if
he did: I'd worked out a little speech in my head for it, and
everything."

To Jude's relief, it was Aisling and not Jason who
answered the intercom and let her inside. Though that
relief quickly evaporated when she actually *saw* her daughter, for the first time in almost a year.

"She'd lost so much weight – her clothes were hanging
off her. There were dark circles under her eyes too, and a
puffiness to them that made it look like she'd been crying.
My first thought when she opened the door to me was that
she'd been ill, or she *was* ill, but she hadn't wanted anyone
to know, so she'd kept it from me.

"She denied it, though, when I asked her. Insisted everything was fine, when I could see otherwise, because I wasn't bloody blind. Even the way she moved seemed a bit off, while she was milling around making the tea. Tense and stilted. It sounds mad, but it was like she was walking the same way she'd been texting: careful, like she was watching every step. *He* wasn't in, so it wasn't that she was doing it for his benefit, or so I thought. Obviously, now, I'm inclined to think he'd just conditioned her to be so cautious, so nervous of putting a foot wrong that she was walking like that and talking like that automatically, even when he wasn't around to keep an eye on her."

And then Jude saw the bruises on her daughter's arms.

"She leaned over to pass me my tea, and the sleeves of her top rode up to show her forearms. They were covered in bruises, elbow to wrist: fresh ones, blue and black, and fading yellow ones she must've had for a while. I think I might have gasped out loud, looking at them. I couldn't help it."

Aisling denied that the bruises were the result of anything but her own clumsiness. But Jude was unconvinced.

"She said she kept hitting herself on the chest of drawers in their bedroom – that Jason had moved them into an awkward position near the bed, and she'd been banging her arms on them whenever she got up. Total bollocks, obviously. My Ash was never clumsy. And she was so *scared*, even as she was spinning me what we both knew was a pack of lies. Just absolutely terrified that I'd seen them, the bruises, and that I must've known what they meant."

That Jason had given Aisling the bruises was, for Jude, a foregone conclusion.

"I didn't even ask her – if it was him, you know. If he'd done that to her. I didn't need to. You put those bruises together with everything else, all those texts and her looking so fragile and the fact she was scuttling around her own flat like a frightened ghost, and it paints a pretty bloody damning picture, doesn't it? So, no, I didn't bother interrogating her. Just put my arms around her and told her to pack a bag, because she was coming home with me.

"And I really think she would have, right then. Would have left him, I mean. Knowing I was there, and she was safe and had somewhere to go... I think it would've given her the confidence to do it. If *he* hadn't chosen that exact second to come flying through the front door."

Jason was, Jude says, extremely surprised to find his mother-in-law in the kitchen of his flat – a surprise that quickly turned to anger when Jude confronted him about the harm he'd been causing her daughter.

"You hear people talk about abusers letting the mask slip. That moment, you know, when they forget they're supposed to act like human beings, and you get a glimpse of the monster underneath. And it was like that, exactly like that. As if, when he first walked in, he'd been just another man, someone you wouldn't look at twice in the street... and then suddenly he was something else completely. Something almost... demonic. Just this cauldron of rage and hatred and disgust, bubbling under the skin of what was supposed to be a person.

"I was so angry myself at what he'd done, and so carried away shouting at him, I didn't think much about it while it was happening. But when I look back on it, I believe he could easily have killed *me* then, if he'd had a bit less self-control. He wanted to, I'll tell you that. You could see it, how *much* he wanted to."

Instead, Jason simply demanded Jude leave the flat and not come back.

"I told him that wasn't going to happen, that I wasn't going anywhere without my daughter. But then Ash..." Jude stops mid-sentence, to catch her breath and wipe her eyes. "I thought she'd say something back to him, with me there. Or just ignore him, and the two of us would just leave him frothing and steaming in that kitchen. But she didn't. She went and stood next to him and stroked him on the arm, like he was a bucking horse she was trying to calm down before he kicked or bolted. And then she looked at me and told *me* to leave, before I did any more damage."

Jude felt she had no choice but to go.

"I told her I'd be back. That I was her mother, and I'd be back for her. Then I told *him* that if he laid another finger on her before then, I'd go right to the police, but not before I'd knocked seven bells of shit out of him myself.

"And then... I went.

"I still don't know what I thought I'd do once I got home. How I'd get her out of there and away from him. I wasn't really thinking properly about anything in the car, to be honest with you. All I could hear was the blood ringing in my ears.

"But whatever I might've done, called Crimestoppers on him or gone back later with Colin and a bloody baseball bat or... something, it turned out to be a moot point, because Ash had sent a message of her own while I was driving. Not to me, though. To Colin. And it was another of those texts that didn't sound like her. That sounded like *he'd* written it."

Colin Fleetwood died from Covid-19-related pneumonia in 2021. Jude, however, has saved the text in question on her own phone, and in this instance has consented to my reproducing it its entirety.

It reads:

*Hi Col - I'm sorry for dragging you into this, but mum's*

*not given me much of an alternative after the way she behaved tonight.*

*I need you to tell her from me that she's not to contact me anymore. She's not to call or text, and she's not to turn up again on the doorstep uninvited. Jay and I are happy as we are, and we don't need her trying to come between us. It's unwanted and it's toxic.*

*I'd appreciate it if you could also tell her that we're moving shortly, so we won't be at the flat after this weekend even if she does decide to make a fool of herself by going where she's not wanted.*

*Mum will ask for the address, but I won't be giving it out. All you need to know is that it's safe, and it's a nice place out in the countryside. A real community that aligns with our values and the way we want to live and bring up our own kids.*

*I'm sorry things have turned out like this, but as I say, she's given me no alternative.*

*Take care,*

*Aisling*

"There aren't words for how it made me feel, reading that," Jude tells me. "I wanted to go back to the flat there and then. It was Colin who persuaded me otherwise, who tried to get me to calm down before I went in all guns blazing. And he was probably right to do that. He couldn't have known how things would play out, could he?

"I tried to call her, though. Right away. You can probably guess she didn't answer. After a few tries, I started going straight through to her voicemail and stopped getting those delivery notifications for the texts I was sending her. I didn't know what the hell that meant, but Colin was a bit more tech-savvy than I was, and he thought she might've blocked me. Barred my number, so it wouldn't even show up on her phone."

On Colin's advice, Jude waited several days before returning to Jason's apartment in Nottingham. By which time, she discovered after speaking to their neighbours, Aisling and Jason had already moved out.

Jude was heartbroken.

"I didn't know what I was supposed to do, after that," she says. "So, I just... kept waiting. Waiting and waiting, for months and months and months. Driving myself mad about it: worrying about where she was, what *he* was doing to her. Whether she was safe. I felt so helpless, so absolutely helpless. Colin wanted me to see a counsellor, towards the end. Maybe I should've done."

Ultimately, Jude *did* seek professional help – not from a therapist, but from a private investigator, who tracked Jason and Aisling down to their new address at the Heart of Solomon.

"He was brilliant, I have to say. Very thorough. He didn't just find out where they'd gone, he typed up a whole report on what that bloody place was and why those bastard Taylors had set it up. I didn't believe him at first, that somewhere like that would even exist in this country. It's such an *American* proposition, isn't it? But exist it did, and barely half an hour away from here.

"You know what I kept coming back to, though, when I was reading that report? It was to that text, the one Ash sent Colin that night. What she'd said about where they were moving; the way she'd described it. *A real community that aligns with our values.*

"And it just... it made no sense to me. No sense. Because since when was *any* of what those Taylors and their woman-hating cult stood for, anything to do with what *my* little girl believed?"

The investigator advised Jude against going directly to the Heart of Solomon herself. The Taylors, he told her, were extremely protective of the privacy of their pseudo-compound, and Nadine Taylor had a history of lashing out at her perceived enemies through the courts and her solicitors. It was, he suggested, very likely they – or Jason himself – would have Jude arrested for trespassing, were she to visit unannounced.

"I didn't know whether to listen to him. I mean, I agonised over it – whether I should go there or not, try to infiltrate their bloody Peoples Temple HQ.[2] It wasn't that I was afraid to get arrested, you know? What were the police going to do to me that could possibly have been worse than losing my only child? But I thought, if I went, and *he* saw me before I could get through to Ash... it might make things worse for *her*.

"And while I was sitting on my hands fretting about all that... *it* happened. And I bloody lost her anyway, didn't I? I lost her for good."

Here a visibly distressed Jude calls a temporary halt to our interview. When we reconvene, I ask her to clarify what she meant by her earlier comment about Jason being responsible for Aisling's death.

"He killed her," she says, with absolute certainty. "I don't know how he did it, but he killed her. Jason Wilson murdered my girl."

But Jason *also* died at the Heart of Solomon, I remind her, as gently as I can. Doesn't that suggest the involvement of a third party?

---

2.  This analogy hit quite close to home, I have to say.

"So maybe he got someone else to do his killing for him. Maybe he planned to hurt Ash and the rest of them and then run off, but something went wrong – or he rubbed the wrong person up the wrong way – and he ended up dead himself. I don't know. I've got a lot of theories. But he did it. If you'd seen the way he looked at me back at that flat, the murder in his eyes then, you'd believe he was capable of it."

Are there no other viable suspects at all, as far as she's concerned?

"What, like that Delaney girl everyone thought did it? No. Absolutely not. It was Jason. All Jason."[3]

Why, I ask her, does she think Jason would have done that? Violent and abusive he may have been, but Aisling was his wife; the Taylors and the Coopers were his friends and neighbours. What could possibly have motivated him to murder all five of them?

"Easy," Jude says, and I get the impression she has indeed been fleshing out this theory for a while. "Ash was going to leave him, and he couldn't let her. Did the others try to help her, and turned into collateral damage for their trouble? I don't know. Doesn't sound like something the Freddie Taylors of the world would do, but who's to say one of that four didn't have a change of heart somewhere, or see Jason doing something to Ash that even *they* couldn't turn a blind eye to?

"But here's the thing: I know a lot more than I used to about domestic violence and coercive control. I know a lot about Jason and the men out there like him. When someone tries to take away what's theirs, or what they *think* is theirs,

---

3.  Rebecca Cooper's former partner Shannon Delaney was briefly considered a suspect by police, but was quickly exonerated – though not before significant damage had been done to her reputation.

even when it's a person, and that person tries to take *herself* off somewhere... they get nasty. Really bloody nasty. It all comes flooding out, all the poison they've been keeping pent up behind the mask. *Pouring* out of them like a rain of fire, burning anyone who gets in its way."

"JOANNA"

For me, as for the many other journalists and documentary-makers who've sought to understand exactly what happened to the Wilsons, the Taylors and the Coopers in September 2019, the opacity of the Heart of Solomon settlement and its workings has proven problematic. Put simply: the insularity of the community – coupled with the Taylors' well-documented propensity for threatening legal action against their critics, and those they perceived as enemies of the Tradwife movement – means we know very little, even now, of how the community actually functioned, day-to-day.

I'd hoped at the outset of this project to plug some of these information gaps by speaking directly to a few of the Heart of Solomon's surviving former residents – those who moved away in the wake of the murders. However, almost none were willing to talk to me; most elected not to reply to my introductory emails or respond to my follow-up enquiries.

With the exception of Joanna.

There are several things the reader should know about

Joanna, before I delve into the conversations we had together on the day we met.

Firstly, Joanna isn't her actual name, but rather a pseudonym we agreed on early in our correspondence, to protect her and her family's privacy. Joanna's privacy is paramount: since leaving the Heart of Solomon, she and her husband have disavowed the Tradwife movement and its values, and they would rather their new colleagues, friends and neighbours not know they were ever a part of it. Joanna, in fact, now considers both the wider "trad" movement and the Heart of Solomon specifically as manifestations of a kind of cult into which she and her husband were indoctrinated – "brainwashed," as she puts it. She has fought hard to, in her words, "deprogram" herself. Though the very particular details of her story will, by her own admission, make her immediately recognisable to any ex-Heart of Solomon residents who read this book in its final, published form, she hopes to avoid the stigma her prior association with the community might bring to her, her husband and their young son in the lives they've built since.

The second thing to know about Joanna is that neither she nor her husband were actually living at the Heart of Solomon at the time of the murders, but had relinquished their cottage three weeks previously, in August 2019 – for reasons that will become apparent to readers as this chapter progresses.

The third is that Joanna knew — and was friendly with — Aisling Wilson in the months preceding Aisling's death, and has been able to confirm what Jude Driscoll only suspected: that Jason Wilson was physically and emotionally abusive towards his wife, and that Aisling was subject to acts of coercive control that Jason made little effort to hide in the comparatively forgiving Heart of Solomon enclave.

Joanna is thirty-five or thereabouts; tall, dark-haired, olive-skinned and curvaceous, her pin-up's figure accentuated by a cinched-waisted vintage summer dress that calls to mind sock hops, polio epidemics and drive-in movie theatres in the American Midwest. Like her husband, whom we agreed to call Dave, she works in marketing, and like him she commands a salary that places her in one of the UK's higher tax brackets. She is articulate, intelligent, and holds an advanced degree in a social science discipline from a well-respected Russell Group university.

She is – though perhaps this is only a reflection of my prejudices and preconceptions – not the sort of woman I would expect to have found succour in the Tradwife movement.

"No?" she says, when I mention this. "I'm not sure I'd agree. I think we're all more susceptible than we think when someone offers us a magic bullet – something that sounds like the solution to all our problems. Much more susceptible, if we tell ourselves we're too smart to be taken in by a cult or a con. If we think we're too clever to be fooled, then our defences are down, and we're vulnerable, because something like that would never work on *us*. Until it does."

Joanna's own journey into the inner reaches of the Tradwife cult began fairly innocuously, propelled by her love of retro fashion and fascination with 1940s and '50s Americana.

"I'd always been into that look," she tells me. "Stockings and petticoats, neckerchiefs and swing dresses, rotary phones and jukeboxes... you name it. Most of the Instagram and Pinterest accounts I followed were vintage-themed. I used to spend hours browsing through them at work, saving and screenshotting things I liked the look of and then trying to find them on Etsy and eBay. I should be embarrassed to admit it, really, but it was kind of an obsession."

Around 2016, Joanna became aware of a sea change in the type of content the social media algorithms were showing her: the fashion and Women's Institute pastiche accounts increasingly interspersed with uploads from recipe inspiration accounts, online Bible study groups for women and, especially, homemakers and self-proclaimed "traditional wives."

"It *is* embarrassing, actually. Because I look back on it, and it's blindingly obvious what I fell into was a radicalisation pipeline. It's the same thing we talk about when we warn kids not to get involved with the sort of content, or sign up to the sort of forums, that might make them want to join ISIS or a neo-Nazi cell, or that might turn them into angry incels shooting at women in the street. That sounds extreme, but the mechanism, it's the same: algorithms owned by tech companies that want to keep you on the hook, feeding you what amounts to propaganda 24/7. Only in my case they wrapped the radicalism in a pair of nylons and tied it up with bobby pins."

Joanna might not, she confesses, have been as receptive to the Tradwife content and its underlying message, had her professional and personal lives been happier. As it was, she found herself more and more bewitched by the promise of a slower pace of life and a calm, domestic bliss facilitated by the embrace of more traditional gender roles.

"I was knackered," she says. "Spent – just completely exhausted. Working twelve-hour days and bursting into tears at my desk, I was so tired. Dave was the same. We'd only been married a year then, and I loved him to death, but there was none of that newlywed energy you'd think there would have been. We were barely seeing each other. Having sex maybe once a month if we could stay awake for it, eating nothing but packets of crisps and ready meals... it wasn't healthy. It wasn't *working*. Not the relationship, because we really did love each other, but the way we were living.

"We'd talk about selling the house and getting out of London, going somewhere quieter. But everywhere we looked at seemed a bit *too* remote for us. And I wasn't sure I fancied our chances of getting jobs in our industry that paid us decent money if we moved outside the M25."

The Tradwives of Instagram seemed, by comparison, to be living the dream: for Joanna, their beautifully arranged kitchens, carefully matched vintage outfits, and the seemingly copious amounts of free time that enabled them to cook, clean and showcase their homes online looked to her nothing less than aspirational.

"So, one day I just... bit the bullet," she says, with an awkward laugh. "I told Dave I wanted to stop working and stay at home, so I could look after him."

To say Dave was shocked would be an understatement.

"I showed him a budget breakdown I'd put together, of how we could make it work financially. And it was doable. Tight, but doable, especially if I cooked everything from scratch. We'd be saving about £500 a month just on my commute. But Dave wasn't sure. I mean, he was supportive, sort of. He'd seen how frazzled I was, and I think he knew himself I was at the end of my rope in terms of what I could handle, workwise. It just scared him a bit, the pressure of having to be the sole breadwinner. He wasn't a particularly traditional bloke, then, and he hadn't seen *me* as being particularly traditional, either. I don't think it ever occurred to him before that day that I might want to give up my career to stay at home and be a housewife."

Nevertheless, Dave agreed to the plan, albeit with some reservations. Joanna left her job and at first, the new arrangement seemed to work for them both.

"Honestly? I loved it. It really *was* more chilled – I could feel all the stress I'd built up draining out of me. And there was all this free time suddenly, even *with* me taking charge of the housework and the cooking and cleaning. I started to feel like myself again. I got my energy back, started taking care of myself the way I used to when I was younger: eating well, looking after my skin, everything. Our sex life picked up as well, which was a nice bonus. I found myself missing him when he went off to the office – so when he came back, I'd be all over him, practically pulling him into bed. He didn't complain about *that*, as you can imagine."

And over time, seeing the positive changes in his wife and marriage, Dave too became an advocate of more tradi-tional divisions of labour within the home.

"I mean, *obviously* he did," Joanna tells me with a smile. "More sex, clean laundry, dinner on the table, no-one nagging him to pick up after himself... it's the dream. It made him... God, I don't even like calling it this, after every-thing, but it made him a better husband. More thoughtful, more romantic. He started bringing me flowers, sending me texts from work reminding me he loved me. And if you knew Dave, you'd know romantic gestures really *aren't* his style."

Joanna, meanwhile, was falling ever deeper down the online Tradwife rabbit-hole.

"There were some girls I got friendly with from this Facebook group we were in, A Woman's Touch – which I realise, yes, sounds like somewhere you'd go for a no-strings lesbian hook-up, but you don't think about how ridiculous things like that sound when you're in them, do you? They were American, all of them. All Tradwives, all stay-at-home like me. From Montana, Texas, Virginia... places like that. Nice girls, mostly."

What did they talk about? I ask her.

"Did we talk politics, you mean?" she replies, sensing where my question is heading. "No. Never. The group had, *has*, a strict *No Politics* rule, so you don't discuss anything like that in the threads, and it kind of... rubbed off on the way we interacted one-on-one. Do I think they were mostly Republicans and Trump supporters? Yeah, for sure. They were all Christians, mostly from red states, and obviously they had pretty traditional values, so you do the math. But they never *said* it. Which meant, you know... I didn't have to think about it. We were more about other stuff, housewife stuff: recipes and cooking, how to get stains out of the carpet, the best places to get a polka dot fit-and-flare for a bargain." She wrinkles her nose. "*Wholesome* stuff."

It was one of these "nice girls" who alerted Joanna to the newly launched Heart of Solomon project.

"She knew Nadine [Taylor]. Knew *of* her. And she'd heard Nadine and her fella were setting up this place in Nottingham, a community for *people like us*: stay-at-home wives and husbands who worked. She and I had talked about me and Dave wanting to move to the countryside but never taking the plunge, and she knew how I felt about us being basically stuck in London. She thought I'd be into it, the Solomon thing. And... she was right, I guess."

Joanna, until now drily ironic and prone to self-mockery in describing her experiences, turns introspective.

"I probably *wouldn't* have been into it, if she'd asked me

at any other time, any other point in my life. And I'm not shifting the blame, *at all*. I did it, I moved us there. That's all on me. But so many of my friends had been so *judgey* about the housewife thing, and my sisters as well: making cracks about sex robots and Stepford Wives, and telling me I was letting the side down and that Dave was taking advantage of me, when all along it had been *my* idea to stop working. So... I suppose there was a bit of an element of *fuck you*, you know what I mean? Like: obviously none of you lot, who are supposed to love me and care about me, *actually* respect me or my decisions here... so maybe I should go somewhere where I know there'll be people who *do*. People who get what I'm about."

The site's bucolic setting didn't hurt, either.

"It looked gorgeous in the photos on the website. That was how I managed to persuade Dave to email Freddie and book an appointment for us to look around – by showing him the pictures of the fields and the cottages. He was... *a bit sceptical* is probably putting it mildly. He didn't see why we'd want to move out to a planned community a hundred miles away to live next door to a bunch of weirdos – or who he *thought* would be a bunch of weirdos. He had it in his head that they'd be Amish types, you know? Forsaking tech-nology and the modern world so they could tend crops and raise barns and whatever.[1] He was quite... well, pleasantly

---

1. Not an unreasonable assumption on her part, to be honest. A lot of cults demonise and/or take a Neo-Luddite approach to digital tech – espe-cially when it comes to devices principally designed for communication. (Ask me how I know...) It's a social-control mechanism, obviously: limit who your members can speak with, and what wider cultural signals they're exposed to, and you're much better equipped to keep a handle on their desires, their aspirations... and their behaviour. Even more so these days, when it's hard to go anywhere – much less buy anything – without a phone in your hand.

surprised when he met Freddie and Nadine and a few of the other guys who'd moved in already, and they seemed... normal. Or they *looked* normal. Like... wearing jeans and trainers, and talking about the football.

"And they were so *nice*. So friendly, like they really *were* a community. It was... sort of lovely, to be honest. A really welcoming place. They didn't try the hard sell on us – not even Freddie, who you'd think would've been into that. But when we got into the car to drive back to London that evening, I was already planning the logistics of how we could do it, how we could move there: how we could rent out the flat to pay the lease on the cottage and still have some left over, and how Dave could fix it so he could work remotely most of the week. He barely needed persuading by then. The countryside and the scenery had done most of the heavy lifting for me. I'm sure he had visions of us getting a dog and taking it out for walks in the fields, and him going fishing and cycling with his new mates on Saturdays, then stopping for a couple of pints in some beer garden on the way home. The absolute polar opposite of supermarket sushi at your desk and shoving past commuters on Black-friars Bridge every night."

The timing of the proposed move was also a factor, Joanna concedes. She and Dave had discovered just a few weeks before the visit that they were expecting their first child – a child neither had any desire to raise in London.

"We didn't mention I was pregnant to Freddie and Nadine when we applied to move in," she says. "It was so early on, we hadn't even had the 12-week scan, and it didn't seem fair to tell them before we told my mum and dad, or Dave's parents. Besides, they'd made a big deal of Solomon being family-friendly and great for kids, so we assumed it wouldn't be an issue... that they'd be happy about it, when they found out."

Their application was accepted, and within weeks, Joanna and Dave had relocated. Their new neighbours were as pleasant and as welcoming as they'd been at that first meeting, and – as Joanna tells it – all progressed smoothly and happily for her and Dave in those first few weeks: the couple assimilating well into the enclave, befriending their co-residents – the Taylors and Aisling Wilson among them – and enjoying the Heart of Solomon's particular slice of scenic rural England every bit as much as they'd hoped they would.

Of the sixteen adults then present in the community, it was only *Jason* Wilson about whom Joanna had doubts.

"I didn't like him. At all, actually. Nor did Dave. He was... you know one of those guys who hits on you when you're out, and he's good-looking and confident, and he seems nice enough, but when you tell him *no* he gets really nasty, and starts calling you names and telling you you'd be lucky to have him but he'd never touch an ugly bitch like you anyway? He reminded me of one of those. For all the criticisms I could throw at *traditional marriage* and the whole cult built up around it, and for all the problems there turned out to be with Solomon... I don't think most of the men there actually hated women. Freddie was a grifter, and there was obviously a lot of what I'd think of now as systemic misogyny built into the foundations of the place... but mostly the blokes were just normal guys, who maybe skewed more conservative than average. I never felt *unsafe* around any of them, in the beginning. Except Jason."

Why?

"He used to hit Aisling. She never said anything about it, at least not to me or Dave, but I saw the bruises on her.

The finger-marks on her wrists and the scratches down her throat she tried to cover up with turtlenecks and scarves. And I saw the way he was with her, when we were all out together – when Freddie and Nadine did a barbecue or held one of their Saturday night dinners. Controlling; *massively* controlling. Monitoring how much she drank, calling her fat if he thought she was eating too much… He'd pretend it was a joke between them, that he was only taking the piss, but nobody talks like that to their partner if they actually respect them, do they? She was a really sweet girl, Aisling, really kind and thoughtful – she could be really funny, too, when you got her on her own – but Jason just… ground her down. He got off on doing it, I think."

The similarities between this and the description of Jason and Aisling's relationship offered by Jude Driscoll are striking – and seem to firmly corroborate Jude's account of Jason's abuse. Did Joanna or her husband ever intervene, I ask – or ask Freddie and Nadine, as the de facto monarchs of the Heart of Solomon, to do so?

"Dave had a word with Freddie." Joanna shakes her head, seeming to chastise herself for her past failings. "And Freddie said *he'd* have a word with Jason – that he'd make it clear that kind of behaviour wasn't acceptable at Solomon, and Jason needed to sort himself out. But other than that… no, we didn't. Aisling was lovely, but we weren't close, and Dave and I had a lot on our plates, with the baby on the way and morning sickness kicking my arse in the first trimester. So, I'm sorry to say: no, we didn't do much at all. We *should've* done, no doubt about it. But we didn't. And I'll regret that 'til I die."

When Joanna and Dave did eventually disclose their pregnancy to others in the Heart of Solomon community, the response was as uniformly positive as she'd anticipated

– with their neighbours, Freddie and Nadine included, flocking to help and dispense wisdom to the parents-to-be. Joanna would regularly receive gifts of home-baked bread, cakes, beef stews and pot roasts from the other Solomon wives; Nadine, whose own children were still relatively young, donated a cot for the couple's nursery, and sent Freddie round to their cottage to assemble it. All of this confirmed for Joanna that she and Dave had made the right decision in moving out of London, to immerse themselves in this strange but gentle and apparently mutually supportive new world.

Which made what happened immediately after the birth of their son that much harder for her to bear.

"Everything was brilliant until we brought him home. Until we started showing him off to people, to Freddie and Nadine, and they saw what he looked like. *Then* things changed. A whole lot of things."

Joanna is referring here, obliquely, to her son's skin colour: a khaki brown that is, I see from the pictures of the now-school-aged child Joanna shows me on her phone, several shades darker than her own. Joanna's father is of Afro-Colombian heritage; her son, she tells me, is his spitting image. Joanna, conversely, more closely resembles her mother, a light-skinned Caucasian woman of Finnish and Belgian descent.

"Freddie and Nadine, they didn't know my Dad was Black," she says. "We hadn't *not* told them, obviously. But how often do you talk about your parents – about your parents' ethnicity – with people who don't know them, and who are only just getting to know *you*? It didn't come up. And Mum and Dad had moved out to a smallholding in the Hebrides after Mum retired, so it's not like they'd been to visit us yet – we were going to go over and see them, when

[Joanna's son] was old enough to travel. I didn't realise..."
She hesitates. "It didn't occur to me that I'd been *passing*.
That passing was something people did anymore in this
country. Or needed to do."

Nadine's reaction, on seeing Joanna and Dave's son for
the first time, left Joanna so taken aback that her voice trem-
bles even as she recalls it.

"She looked down at [the baby] in his Moses basket,
then up at me and Dave, then down again at [the baby], and
she said in that bloody Scarlett O'Hara accent: "Well, now –
how do you suppose *that* happened?" She was sort of
laughing when she said it, but not *really* laughing, you
know? Like she'd seen something that had given her a
massive shock, but she knew she had to cover it up, make a
joke out of it.

"I wasn't even sure what she was getting at initially. I'd
only been out of hospital a day and I was in such a daze I
barely knew who I was, so what she was trying to say... it
didn't really register. It was Dave I think who asked her
what she meant. And then she just... she did that laughing
thing again. And she said, like it was blindingly obvious: "I
*mean*, that child's a little darker than he ought to be, isn't
he?" And *then* I got it. What she meant was: *what's a nice
white couple like you doing with a baby like* that?

"I just... I started crying. I don't remember much else
beyond that: everything was so raw anyway, so completely
surreal, my body didn't feel like it was mine and I hadn't
really slept properly since [her son] arrived, so when she
said that... she might as well have punched me.

"Dave dealt with it, thank God. I don't know what he
said to her – I'd sort of zoned out by then – but she left
pretty quickly after, and she didn't come 'round to the
cottage again. I wanted to ask him about it, but the way he

looked after he'd seen her out made me think maybe it wasn't something *either* of us really wanted to talk about. I just let him put his arms around me until I'd cried myself out."

Growing up in a liberal and well-to-do area of a large multicultural city, and living and working thereafter in London, Joanna had been lucky – she tells me – to have experienced comparatively little overt racism prior to her immersion in the Heart of Solomon.

"I realise I was coming from a place of privilege," she says. "And I suppose on some level I must have seen how white it all was – not just Solomon, but the whole Trad-wife... thing. I guess I just didn't see it as deliberate, so much as something that had... worked out that way. I mean, think about where a lot of the girls in that Facebook group come from, the demographic composition of those US states. Somewhere like Montana's not exactly known for its cultural diversity, is it? So, it stood to reason their movement was going to skew a bit whiter than it would have if it had started in Bradford or Brixton. I assumed the whiteness was a by-product. Not that racism was, you know... the whole point.

"I know better now, obviously. It's sort of hard to kid yourself otherwise when your neighbours start to shun you because your new-born's too brown for them to look at without wincing."

That word, *shunning*, seems to neatly encapsulate Joanna's explanation of her family's treatment at the hands of the Heart of Solomon community, after Nadine's visit.

"I'm not sure how else you'd describe what happened. People just... stopped talking to us. Nobody came 'round to see us or say hello to [her son]. Nobody invited us to any more of the barbecues or the dinners, and those were *defi-*

*nitely* still going on – we could smell them when we opened the windows at the weekends, hear the noise of people talking in Nadine and Freddie's back garden. And, okay, maybe you could say, *they didn't think you'd want to come, with a new baby* – but that doesn't account for why nobody popped in to see how we were, does it? Or why people would ignore us and scuttle away if we saw them on the street and waved hello when we took [the baby] out in the pram.

"No, it was deliberate. Definitely it was deliberate. And it was Nadine's doing, hers and Freddie's. We had an idea then that was the case – it was the only thing that made sense, after how she'd reacted to [the baby]. Dave misread the situation a bit, of course: he thought Nadine might have been spreading it around that [the baby] wasn't his, and *that* was why they were all behaving the way they were – that they saw me carrying another man's child as me spitting in the face of their traditional values. Sounds crazy, but then... it's less crazy than *they dropped you because you weren't white enough for them*, isn't it?

"Less crazy now, I guess. Now we all know a bit more about Nadine and Freddie and that Gorecki guy. And that whiteness maybe *was* the point of Solomon, after all."

I'd like to offer some further perspective on this last statement: that is, to contextualise the racist underpinnings of the Heart of Solomon community to which Joanna refers.

Doing this, however, requires me to briefly suspend the transcription of my conversation with Joanna in order to explore and summarise the connections between the Trad-wife movement, the American Christian Nationalism ethos and the "Great Replacement." That is: the far-right conspiracy theory that points to a rise in Black and brown populations in the US and Europe as "evidence" that white populations are being systematically bred out and "replaced" by non-white equivalents.

It also requires me to introduce a man whose public profile and manifesto have cast a long and somewhat intimidating series of shadows over the House of Solomon murders and the investigations that followed: Freddie Taylor's long-time friend and former collaborator, the currently incarcerated White Nationalist agitator Jerzyk "George" Gorecki.

GEORGE GORECKI

"Traditional marriage" may not be inherently white – or indeed inherently white supremacist – for all of its conservative proponents. But with high-profile Tradwives like Karla Mayne urging fans to "love and honour their European roots" on their Instagram pages, and influencers like Hallie Osterley imploring fellow Tradwives on TikTok to "make white babies" in the spirit of preventing an imagined "white genocide," it's hard to deny that *some* connection exists between #Tradlife and the racist ideology and rhetoric of the 21st century alt-right.

Osterley's campaign to accelerate the production of "white babies," for example, speaks directly to the Great Replacement theory: the widespread belief amongst alt-right conspiracists – disseminated globally across innumerable Red Pill-inspired Reddit forums and fomented in the US by commentators from former Fox News host Thad Brady to Republican congresswoman Jeanie Hesse – that white Europeans and Americans of white European extraction risk "extinction" and "replacement" by non-white races in the coming decades.

This "extinction" they regard as the logical outcome of a confluence of social-cultural determinants, ranging from large-scale immigration (of African, Asian and Middle Eastern nationals into European and US regions) and the legalisation of abortion and same-sex marriage, to declining birth rates amongst white European and American populations (versus Black and brown equivalents) and the rise of interracial relationships. All of which, for those of a white supremacist inclination, equate to a partial or total loss of "indigenous" European cultural identity. Only through the intervention of young, fertile white men and women, they argue – only through the willingness of these men and women to create as many white babies as they're physically able – can this apocalyptic event be averted.

Nadine Taylor, as we'll see in later chapters, was no stranger to the Great Replacement theory – associating for a time with members of the nativist, radical-right group Chosen Christians in her home state of Florida, before relocating to the UK and continuing to espouse white nationalist and white evangelical talking points in conversation until her death. Joanna's suspicions – that Nadine was a racist who sought to create, in the Heart of Solomon, a kind of traditionalist whites-only utopia, and expand it with brood upon brood of Caucasian babies – were likely all too accurate a reflection of Nadine's privately held opinions.

*Freddie* Taylor also had a history of racist thought and action. Not least via his once-close friendship with George Gorecki, leader of the now-defunct Whites For Whites (W4W) Alliance: a single-issue pressure group dedicated, as per its now-archived online manifesto, to "the removal of non-whites from our [British] shores" and "the restoration of a truly British white sovereignty."

Measured against the swastika-tattooed, football hooligan-esque neo-Nazis and white power agitators apt to storm the Cenotaph on Remembrance Sunday, Gorecki is atypical, to say the least. The son of Polish immigrants, and an avowed vegan and straight-edge teetotaller, he was born in Ealing, West London in 1982 and raised in the area, attending an ethnically diverse local comprehensive where he was, according to those who knew him there in the 1990s, a self-identified socialist and die-hard fan of the anti-capitalist rap/metal outfit Rage Against The Machine.[1] He parlayed early interests in web design and programming into a degree in media technologies. And it was in his second year of university—as cultural theorist Hamza Rashid writes in a recent study of the British far-right—that Gorecki, inspired by Francis Galton's eugenics, Charles Murray's Bell Curve and an encounter with the American white supremacist William Pierce's racist and antisemitic *Turner Diaries*, began to embrace "white pride," forging for himself a new political identity based around neo-fascist ideals of ethnic nationalism and racial separatism, anti-feminism, Islamophobia and an extreme Euroscepticism.[2] The latter of these would, ironically, come to be assimilated into the UK political mainstream in the run-up to — and wake of — the 2016 Brexit vote.

In 2004, while working as an IT technician for an environmental charity in Slough, Gorecki founded the website which would go on to become Jackboot: at one stage the largest and most active neo-Nazi forum in the UK. Using the handle Radegast, Gorecki – as webmaster and lead

1. Lansdowne, A. (2019) *Robinson, Collett, Smith & Gorecki: The Remaking of the British Far Right.* London: Big Tent, pp76-120.
2. Rashid, H. (2022) *A Homegrown Technofascism: Where The Far-Right Go To Plan A Riot.* London: Blind Justice.

forum moderator – grew Jackboot's numbers to a purported 30,000 members.[3] On his watch, the Jackboot community organised protests and rallies at events including the opening of the Harpenden United Synagogue in Hertfordshire, the 50th anniversary celebration of the Dudley Women's Centre, and, in 2006, the funeral of murdered Sikh teenager Amandeep Singh Sanghera.

Freddie Taylor, then a history and politics tutor at a further education college in Norwich, was a keen participant in Jackboot forum discussions; his username, WesternRationalist, a nod to his enthusiasm for the philosophy, ideals and "civilisation" of a bygone Europe. Unsurprisingly, it was Freddie's Jackboot contributions that brought him to Gorecki's attention – and through their interactions on the platform that the two became friends, first online and subsequently in person.

Despite Freddie Taylor's insistence when questioned in interviews that the pair had drifted apart prior to Gorecki's founding of the W4W Alliance in 2010, and that their friendship had disintegrated altogether by Gorecki's conviction in 2014 for the racially aggravated manslaughter of bartender Kelvin Thomas, there can be no question that the men were once close: Freddie, as Rashid observes, served as an usher at Gorecki's 2008 wedding to his (now ex) wife Hazel Tipton, and went on to deliver a ten-minute speech at the reception.[4]

We'll return in later chapters to Freddie Taylor's relationship with Gorecki and the British far-right, as well as to Nadine Taylor's involvement with the Chosen Christians in the USA.

---

3. Ibid.
4. Ibid.

The Gorecki link alone, however, is enough to suggest there is indeed a clear trajectory to be traced from the racist white nationalist precepts of groups like Jackboot and W4W to the "traditional" values of Freddie Taylor's Heart of Solomon project – however strongly *both* Taylors may have claimed otherwise.

"Aisling wasn't like the rest of them. She wasn't racist," Joanna tells me, returning to the original topic of our discussion when I ask her how the Wilsons, particularly, reacted to the "revelation" of her son's ethnicity. "Or... I've got no reason to think she was, I guess. She was the only one of all of them at that place who carried on speaking to us after that thing with Nadine. When Jason wasn't about, anyway. She'd barely look our way when he was – but then, she'd barely look at *anyone* without his permission, so I wouldn't want to infer anything just from that."

It's been suggested, I say – reflecting on my interview with Jude Driscoll – that despite his own demise at the hands of the murderer, Jason might have been inadvertently responsible for the Heart of Solomon killings, or at the very least implicated in them in some way that's yet to come to light. Does Joanna have any thoughts on that hypothesis?

Joanna laughs. "What, like he faked his own death so he could get away with offing the rest of them? Seems a bit far-fetched to me. And the police are pretty confident he *is* actually dead, so I'm going to go along with their assessment,

I think. I don't love the boys in blue, but they've probably got a better handle on the situation than I do." Then, more seriously, she adds: "Jason, though... he definitely *could* have done something like that. To Aisling, anyway. Especially..."

Especially?

Joanna fixes me with a long, level stare, as if deciding whether or not she ought to trust me with the information she's about to impart. "Especially since she was planning to leave him," she says, finally. "Or... she *wanted* to leave him, might be a better way of putting it. I don't think he'd have *let* her go, you know? He wasn't that type."

How, though, I ask her, can she be sure of what Aisling wanted?

"Because she told me."

Soon after their unfortunate encounter with Nadine, and the community ostracism that followed, Joanna and Dave decided to leave the Heart of Solomon, the better to protect their young son and themselves from its hitherto unsuspected racist foundations. One day before their scheduled departure, Joanna – in defiance of the looks and whispers that had kept her indoors in previous weeks – had taken her son for a walk in his pram around the small park that served as the Solomon village green, where she'd bumped into Aisling, who had been jogging around the block. It was the last time the women would see each other.

"Freddie had accepted the notice on our cottage as soon as Dave handed it in. No questions, no argument. He'd been expecting it, we think, probably ever since Nadine went home and told him about [Joanna's son] and what he looked like. We didn't even have to see out the lease: as far as Freddie was concerned, we could pack up our stuff and leave that week. Which is pretty much what we did.

"I assume Aisling heard the news from Nadine or one of

the other women. Gossip travelled about as fast as you'd expect around Solomon. It was actually quite surprising that she stopped and spoke to me, when she saw me: I figured Nadine would've spread the word by then that we were personae non grata. But she *did* speak to me, even though half the wives were probably watching us from behind the curtains in their living rooms.

"I didn't bother with small talk, not when we both knew what the deal was. Just said we'd be leaving tomorrow, and I hoped she looked after herself. And that was when she said it. *I wish I could go with you. Living here is like being in prison.*

" Those were her exact words. And I guess it must have felt like that, for her, with Jason watching her every move and waiting for her to slip up so he could feel justified when he hit her. So, I said, *well, why don't you? Just wait until he goes to work and then walk out the door and don't come back.*

"I didn't need to say who *he* was. Neither of us needed to.

"And she gave me this sad little smile, and shook her head, and said, *He'd kill me. He'd kill me before he'd let me leave him.*

"I started to say something back to her, about how she absolutely *could* leave him if she wanted to, and Dave and I would help her if it came down to it – but she just kept shaking her head, like, *drop it now, please.* So I..." Joanna shakes her own head, regretfully. "I did. And she jogged off, back to her prison cell, to wait for her scumbag of a husband to come home. And the next day *we* were out of there, trying not to dwell on what happened and how we were basically driven out like lepers... and then a few weeks later the murders are all over the news and Twitter, and obviously I was thinking what a lucky escape we'd had, and how that could've been us, but also: that poor, poor girl. Because she never *did* manage to get away, to break out of that prison. She was so scared of what would happen if she tried to leave, she stayed exactly where she was, and she ended up dying anyway. And there's no fucking justice in that, is there? No justice at all."

JASON

Joanna and Jude Driscoll are not the only ones out there who believe Jason Wilson to have blood on his hands. His culpability in the murders of his wife and neighbours – and by extension, somewhat paradoxically, in his own death – has been the subject since 2019 of much heated discussion among online true crime enthusiasts. Many, despite the physical evidence to the contrary, consider him responsible.

Take, for example, this post from Reddit user WakeMe-UpBeforeCthulhu, taken from the subreddit r/heartof-solomon:

**We know he was violent and he was abusing poor Aisling but we're supposed to believe it was a complete stranger that broke in that night and murdered her and everyone else there with her? Sorry but no, not buying it. 100% Jason did it and found a way to make it look like it wasn't him by faking his own death. People do it all the time. Look at that man in the canoe who pretended to go missing in Hartlepool so his wife could claim on the insurance. It took five**

**years for anyone to work out he was still alive. + how hard can it be really to cut off your own hand and leave it as evidence to throw us all off the scent?**

And this reply in the same thread, from user Antifemicida97:

**Oh, for sure. Did you see the interview with his ex in that O'Neill doc? You can't watch that and not think he's the doer**

The interview referenced here features in a segment of last year's Alex O'Neill documentary *121.6 Dead Women* – its title an allusion to the average number of women killed by men every year in Britain. In it, O'Neill speaks with Jason Wilson's former girlfriend, a woman identified pseudonymously as "Ingrid."

Her face hidden in shadow and her voice digitally disguised to conceal her identity, Ingrid recalls at length her three-year relationship with Jason, prior to his marriage to Aisling; a relationship pockmarked by repeated instances of emotional abuse and physical violence, all of them under-girded by Jason's need to control, as she puts it, "every aspect of [her] life, from morning to night." She also describes, in one especially memorable portion of the interview, an alco-hol-fuelled sexual assault to which Jason subjected her following a night out with friends – an assault so trauma-tising it led Ingrid, despite the constant fear and self-doubt with which she then lived, to seek help from a local rape crisis charity, who urged her to file a report with the police.

Though no report was ultimately filed, the incident was enough to spur Ingrid to end the relationship: to resign from her property management job without giving notice and abandon the apartment she shared with Jason while the latter was at work, taking with her nothing but her passport and two suitcases' worth of personal possessions. So worried was she that he would come after her, she claims, she sought refuge with family in Brno, and remained in the Czech Republic for several years thereafter – not returning to the UK until 2019, upon learning of his death.

Jason's abuse, as Ingrid recounts it, is both horribly plausible and, particularly in light of the accounts given by Joanna and Jude Driscoll of his subsequent behaviour towards Aisling, difficult to dispute.

Nevertheless, online commentators in the so-called "manosphere" – a nebulous digital ecosystem of men's rights activists, "involuntary celibate" incels, aggrieved anti-feminists, and other and more disparate misogynist participants – have indeed disputed it: some discrediting Ingrid's testimony while painting Jason as the victim of an anti-male conspiracy to smear his name and reputation in death, and others justifying whatever physical violence he *might* have resorted to as the actions of a desperate, cornered man long abused by aggrieved and vengeful women.

(For a great number of these men, the *sexual* violence of which Jason stands accused is a matter of no consequence. Intimate partner rape, for many in the manosphere, is an impossibility, a contradiction in terms: by consenting to a relationship with a man, they suggest, women have de facto consented to sex with that man whenever he might want it, irrespective of their own desires. *Withdrawing* sex in this context, as user ALionAwakened01 observes in the subreddit r/RealMenTalk, is "like giving someone a gift voucher then telling them they're not allowed to spend it. It's bullshit. She says yes to the relationship and all the benefits that brings her, then she's saying yes to the s3x as well").

Some have gone further still. In the manosphere as in

digital true crime arenas, speculation around what role, if any, Jason might have played in the Heart of Solomon murders continues unabated.

Perhaps surprisingly, a minority of contributors to the innumerable Solomon threads that litter the forums of r/TheRedPill and A Place For Men (APFM) agree that Jason may indeed have been responsible: that he was able, for example, to successfully fake his own death after slaughtering his wife and neighbours, throwing police off the scent and escaping to pastures unknown. He, like Elvis and Lord Lucan before him, has been "spotted" by smartphone-wielding conspiracists in locations from Dakar and Tallinn to the Isle of Wight – though few of the blurred and heavily pixelated images shared of tall white men strolling the streets of Estonia and Senegal bear even a passing resemblance to Jason Wilson circa 2019.

These conspiracies differ from those circulating within (predominantly female) true crime communities, however, in their framing of Jason not as a monster on the run, but as a hero: one who, against all odds, evaded persecution by a pro-feminist UK media and prosecution by a misandrist judiciary.

Yes, these posters argue, he probably did it. But he must, surely, have had his reasons; must have been goaded in some way by his wife, or Nadine Taylor and Rebecca Cooper, or all three. No reasonable man, after all, would stoop to such extreme violence without provocation. Especially not an attractive, successful Alpha male like Jason.

In the words of APFM user BlackPillBadMan:

**Maybe he killed them and maybe he didn't, but you know if he did it was only after one of those bitches [Aisling, Nadine and Rebecca] backed him into a corner. Did anyone even**

**bother asking what THEY might of done to JW [Jason] in the runup to him or whoever unaliving them? Like, maybe Nadz [Nadine] tried it on with him an when he knocked her back she went cray cray and said he tried to rape her or whatever, and FT [Freddie] and BC [Brendan Cooper] believed her so JW didn't have no choice but [to] fuckin tear up the lot of them**

Other APFM users, like Looksmaxxed2DLimit7, have explicitly celebrated Jason for his supposed crimes, comparing him favourably to other misogynistic mass murderers hailed as manosphere icons:

**I don't even care why he did it, man. Taking out those 3 bitches and their cuck husbands was fking EPIC shit. [Lewiston, Maine gym shooter] Danny [Hassbeck] and [Brighton serial rapist] CWP [Chris Wainwright-Porter] epic**

**Whatever it was, they deserved it. Just hope my man Jay is lying on a beach somewhere with a cold beer and more pussy than he knows what to do with**

More common is the manosphere-wide belief in Jason's innocence: that he *didn't* do it and in fact was as much a victim of the real Heart of Solomon killer as Aisling, the Taylors and the Coopers, but has been falsely implicated and retrospectively defamed by a feminist Deep State intent on covering up the true circumstances of the murders.

r/TheRedPill contributor SonOfZeusAndMayhem articulates this position:

**Trad [lifestyles] and Freddie [Taylor]'s work were just starting to get known and talked about**

in the MSM [mainstream media] and some of the sheeple were starting to wake up to how toxic feminism and woke liberalism actually are, so of course someone high up needed to go in and shut it down. Can you think of a better way of destroying Trad and The Message [of traditional antifeminist values] than by taking out its figureheads in one big, bloody chop of the sword?

Then putting another nail in the coffin by pinning the blame for it on one of the husbands, so everyone thinks of horrific male violence whenever they think of Trad?

**Obviously DYOR** [Do Your Own Research – a well-used phrase among online conspiracy theorists]. **But the whole thing smells like PsyOps to me**

References to Freddie Taylor as a "figurehead" of the Tradlife movement, and an alt-right martyr sacrificed on the altar of liberalism, abound across the manosphere.

It feels appropriate therefore that it's to Freddie, and then Nadine, that we now turn in the chapters that follow.

# VICTIMS 3 & 4: FREDDIE & NADINE TAYLOR

# FREDDIE

Much of the public speculation around what we might call the *whodunnit* aspect of the Heart of Solomon murders has centred, as we've seen, on the potential role played by Jason Wilson: a man with a documented history of violent and threatening behaviour, particularly towards women.

We can't begin to understand the context of the murders, however – and perhaps even the motivation *for* them[1] – before first understanding a little about the Heart of Solomon's First Couple, Freddie and Nadine Taylor, without whom (and without whose money, influence and fervently practised belief in the "traditional" family) the community would not have existed at all.

---

1. Helen – is this too much? Too sensationalist? I know I keep saying we're not trying to out a murderer – this isn't fucking Cluedo – but I worry some of the more... editorial sections come off a bit Poirot Gets Elliptical To Build Suspense Before Gathering The Suspects Together In The Library For The Big Denouement. Let me know what you think? We can always tighten things up in the edit – G.

And who, like Jason Wilson, had their secrets.[2]

Freddie Taylor, the Heart of Solomon founder whose own heart was carved out of his body and presented on a dinner plate at the kill site, was born in January 1979, the only child of Bernadette (née Farrier), an Accident & Emergency nurse turned stay-at-home mum, and her late husband Jim, who owned and managed an ice-cream parlour not far from Bournemouth Pier. Growing up in the small seaside suburb of Lathercombe, about a mile north of Boscombe Beach, Freddie was – according to his mother, with whom I was fortunate enough to secure an interview – an introverted and "peaky" child. Despite cultivating interests in boxing, mixed martial arts and strength training later in life, he eschewed the open-water swimming, surfing and water sports beloved of his peers in favour of computer games, fantasy novels (from writers like Terry Brooks and Robert E. Howard), and assembling and decorating an ever-growing collection of miniatures, many of them inspired by the Norse and ancient Germanic pantheons. He was, as Bernadette describes him, "a proper bookworm" who performed well academically at primary and secondary school level; the end-of-year reports she still keeps, handwritten by Freddie's teachers between Years 4 and 9, suggest a keen and intellectually engaged pupil with a particular aptitude for English and humanities subjects.

"He always did his homework, always," Bernadette tells me over a glass of homemade iced tea. The two of us sit in the well-kept Dorset bungalow in which she's lived since marrying Jim in the mid-70s – the same bungalow in which

---

2. Okay... we're definitely heading into *A Netflix True Crime Exclusive* territory now. Will tone it down in the final draft – G.

Freddie was born and raised, until he left for university in 1997.

Freddie's childhood bedroom looks – or so she assures me – much as it did in the 1980s and 90s, down to the shelves of dog-eared mass-market paperbacks and the Sony PlayStation and controllers (complete with bulky 12-inch television) that rest on the carpet: a shrine to a slightly nerdy male adolescence of ages past. I half-convince myself I can still smell the lingering bouquet of Lynx body spray and Hugo Boss cologne in the slightly stale air.

In fact, there is something of the pre-IKEA time capsule about the bungalow, with its mint-green wallpaper, faintly chintzy curtains and floral Laura Ashley three-piece-suite. Even Bernadette herself bears traces of this aesthetic, from her brown knitted dress to her feathered Meg Ryan hair-style and careful blonde highlights.

A curvy, broad-shouldered white woman in what I guess to be her early 70s, though I'm reluctant to ask, Bernadette radiates the kind of sadness you'd expect of someone who's survived not only the violent death of her only son, but a torrent of media scrutiny (and occasionally abuse) directed towards her in the months thereafter.

"Not everyone were kind, when Fred were taken," she says, in her soft West Country dialect. "Those ones who disagreed with what he done, before – they seemed to get a good bit louder about it all when he weren't around to talk back to 'em. And I *were* around, see? I were his mum, so them ones who had a bone to pick with Fred's beliefs... well, they went and picked it with me instead. I don't know how many times I had strangers come up to me in the street to tell me I was a bad mother, and if I'd done a better job of bringing him up maybe then none of what happened *would've* happened."

The beliefs in question – Freddie's oft-professed opinions on modern masculinity, "gender ideology" and, to borrow the title of his 2016 self-help bible, How To Be A Man In A World Gone Batsh**t – were well-known to the general public long before the murders.

His video series Heroes & Masterminds, showcasing the "genius" of some of the "Great Men" of Classical Greco-Roman eras and inspired by his work as a sixth-form college lecturer in History and Politics, went live on the pre-YouTube video-sharing platform Cathode Ray in 2004 – around the same time George Gorecki, with whom Freddie would go on to become close friends, was unleashing his neofascist forum Jackboot on the world. Heroes & Masterminds, it quickly became apparent, was intended predominantly as a star-making vehicle for Freddie and an outlet for the "rationalist," libertarian, antifeminist and Western-supremacist viewpoints to which he subscribed: viewpoints now closely associated with the far-right, the alt-right and the manosphere, and with contemporary talking heads like Canadian academic Jordan Peterson and British commentator and would-be politician Carl Benjamin (better known to his subscribers as Sargon of Akkad).

Each 15-minute episode of Heroes & Masterminds followed a similar format. The opening segment would see the then-twentysomething Freddie, in a starched white shirt and plain beige sweater, deliver a straight-to-camera summary of the ideas and achievements of the particular "Hero" or "Mastermind" of the hour. There would follow a brief montage of images of and quotations from the episode's subject, supplemented by a sombre reading of excerpts from key texts by Freddie himself. Finally, Freddie would deliver his closing statement and suggestions: his own recommendations on ways in which the ideas of each

Great Man could and ought to be incorporated into the practice of contemporary everyday living.

Some of these suggestions were benign, if prosaic: in an episode on Seneca and the Stoics, for example, Freddie concludes that his audience should "do something nice for someone today, but don't stick around to take credit for it. You'll want to, I get it, but that's just your ego talking. Do the thing, then walk away."

Others, however, were more problematic, if in keeping with the misogynist ideologies Freddie would subsequently adopt wholesale. From a reading of Aristotle, he advises male viewers to "keep your guard up around women. They're emotional, impulsive, which means they're gonna lash out at you if you piss them off, whether you were in the wrong or not. They'll lie about you, even. So, you've got to be careful."

"I don't know where all that came from," Bernadette says, of this early casual misogyny. "His dad weren't like that. I wouldn't have called Jim a feminist, definitely wouldn't have gone that far, but he was only ever respectful to women, and he treated me like a queen at home. But an equal too, if you catch what I mean, which was a damn sight rarer then than it is now. I don't know what it was Fred saw to make him think that way, but he didn't see it here."

Where then *did* it come from? How, inasmuch as it's possible to know for certain, does a man like Freddie Taylor – the kind of man driven to create and dedicate his life to the development of a place like the Heart of Solomon – come to exist in the world?

"If I had to put my finger on it, I'd probably tell you it were after Cambridge that it started," Bernadette says, when I press her on the genesis of Freddie's "traditionalist" worldview.

*After Cambridge?* I ask, mildly confused by her response. Freddie, according to all the sources I've consulted, attended the University of Liverpool, not one of the Cambridge colleges – graduating in 2000 with a 2.1 degree in Ancient History and Classical Civilisation.

"He applied to go there, to do Classics. He got an interview at Trinity College, one of the really old fancy ones, and *he* seemed to think it went well right after. But then they turned him down, and he got a bit... funny about things. Bitter, if you're allowed to say that about your own child. Started going on about political correctness, and how the place they should've offered him probably went to a Black boy who'd been predicted 3 Cs or a girl from a state school in Darlington who'd threatened to sue the university for sex discrimination. How it were all about meeting quotas, and eff all to do with talent. I told him that were all a load of rubbish, and that wasn't how a place like Trinity made its decisions, but he weren't about to listen to me. I were only his mum. I didn't go to university, let alone a fancy Cambridge college, so what did *I* know about anything?"

*He said that?*

"Oh, yeah. It got quite nasty between him and me, especially when I reminded him he'd put Liverpool down as his second choice and they'd given him an offer already. *And a lot of Prime Ministers went to Liverpool, did they?* – that was what he said back to me. Right before he stormed off to his room to put his music on and stop up all night playing on that blasted games machine."

*He had political ambitions, even then?*

"Ever since he were little, he'd had them – way, way before the Cambridge business. He were always reading the paper and recording Question Time off the telly, making me listen to the news on the radio whenever we were out in the car. He loved it. I think he were about eight when he first told me he were going to be an MP when he grew up, not long after we'd watched Mrs Thatcher get in again. '87, I suppose that would've been."

In spite of his disappointment, and his failure to matriculate at the alma mater of so many of his political heroes, Freddie continued on to Liverpool, and from there to a teacher training program at what was then the Southampton Institute of Higher Education, just a forty-minute drive from Bournemouth – moving back into the family home, with Bernadette, for financial reasons for the duration of his course.

By which time, as Bernadette tells it, the relationship between mother and son was already somewhat strained.

"He were quite snippy, all that year," she remembers. "Which, do you know what, I can understand. No-one wants to be living at home with their mum at twenty-odd, do they? But it were more than that sometimes, more than just your usual overgrown teenage tantrums when his jeans weren't washed or his dinner weren't ready for him soon as he got in from his teaching. It were more like... everything I said to him were stupid. Not worth listening to, because I hadn't been to college and I couldn't talk to him on his level. He took to saying just that, more or less. *What do* you *know about it?* he'd ask me, when I tried to talk to him about this and that I'd heard on Radio 4. Or *and you're an expert, are you?* if I mentioned something about schools and kiddies while he were looking over his coursework. I oughtn't to say it, but I think both of us were a bit relieved when he finished up at Southampton and took that job in Norwich."

By the mid-2000s, several years into Freddie's teaching job in Norwich and with his Heroes & Masterminds channel taking up much of his time outside of the class-room, the pair were seeing each other only sporadically: at Christmas, and when Freddie would occasionally return to Bournemouth for a one- or two-day visit. Bernadette made the greater effort to maintain contact, phoning and leaving messages for her son at his Costessey flat several times a week; Freddie, however, resisted her every suggestion that she might travel to Norfolk to see him in person. Not once, she says, was she allowed to see the inside of his apartment.

Some of his reluctance to entertain a visit from his mother, it occurs to me, may have sprung from a desire to keep her at arm's length from the company he was keeping; to entirely compartmentalise his family and social lives. As of 2005, we may recall, Freddie was already an ardent contributor to George Gorecki's neo-Nazi Jackboot forum and had formed a firm friendship with Gorecki himself. And, while Freddie was less open with his colleagues and fellow teachers than Gorecki about the specifics of his ever-intensifying interests in white nationalism and antifeminism, and while (perhaps as a consequence of his teaching career) he attended none of the more visible protests and pickets Gorecki organised around this period, we can conclude from the transcripts of their online conversations, as unearthed and analysed by Hamza Rashid, that Freddie's social circle included both other Jackboot members and fellow neo-Nazi sympathisers.[3]

"I never met him," Bernadette says of Gorecki – not defensive, as one might expect, but exhausted, as if she's addressed that particular point too many times before. "And I'd never have wanted to, neither. I know what you must think of me, after what Fred got himself into, but I'm no

---

3.  Rashid, H. *A Homegrown Technofascism*, p159.

racist. My sister June were half Black – bet *that* didn't make it into the papers, did it? Darker'n you, she was.[4] Her real dad were a GI, come over here in the war just long enough to get our mum in trouble. Junie were out working, and then stuck in bed with breast cancer most of the while Fred were growing up, so I'm not saying they were close, but she were his auntie, and I don't know *how* he squared that with hisself while he were palling around with the likes of Gorecki. Cognitive dissonance – isn't that what they call it now?"

Or simple hypocrisy, I consider.[5]

Whatever his motivations, and however he reconciled white power ideology with the facts of his own background, by late 2006 Freddie was a rising star of the right-wing web. Moving his video content from the Cathode Ray platform to YouTube in the summer of that year precipitated an enormous uptick in viewership for Freddie and the Heroes & Masterminds brands, which in turn enabled him to launch a subscription-only website for his fans and followers. The website, Raw Meat, on which could be accessed (for just £9.99 a month) Freddie's musings on the tribulations of the "traditional" man in an increasingly "feminised" world, also allowed him a platform from which to dispense advice on how such men might do everything from choosing a well-cut suit to attracting the attentions of a beautiful woman –

---

4.  Helen - do we cut this, or keep it? I'm not sure *my* ethnicity is really the point here... – G.

5.  Because it often is, isn't it? Racists love to pick a handful of 'good ones' to leverage as exceptions for whatever 'rules' they devise about [x ethnicity]. I daresay my mother's father – may he forever step on upturned Lego blocks in whichever section of the afterlife he's currently occupying – would've thought I was One Of The Good Ones myself, if he'd ever bothered to meet me. And god knows homophobes like to do the same.

and generated sufficient revenue that he was able to retire permanently from teaching in 2007, and to move thereafter to the leafy Southwest London suburb of Teddington.

Sometime around 2006, he also crossed paths online with an American named Nadine Halliday: the woman who would not long afterwards become his wife.

"He didn't tell me anything about her, first off," Bernadette says. "And when he did – when he *had* to, 'cause she were moving over here to live with him – he said they met on one of them dating websites. That... what was it? eHarmony. The *way* he said it, though... I can't say it rang true for me. I thought it might've been the real story were something a bit more embarrassing. Something Fred didn't want anyone knowing, least of all his mum."

In fact, as Freddie and Nadine confirmed in their 2009 YouTube video *Love At First Sight?*, the couple met on a very different dating site: the short-lived US enterprise ConservaDate, which between 2005 and 2010 "[brought] together traditionally-minded folks, across the globe and under God."

While Freddie was initially circumspect about Nadine and their relationship, Bernadette suspects that a solo holiday he took to Orlando in the winter of 2006 was organised with a view to his meeting Nadine, a Florida native, in person. Regardless: by March 2007, the two were engaged, and Freddie had already begun making plans for Nadine's relocation across the Atlantic to Teddington.

Just as Jude Driscoll once harboured doubts about her future son-in-law, however, so Bernadette, too, had reservations about Nadine.

"She were... well, she were perfectly pleasant, when Fred brought her down here to see me. Very polite, nice manners, well put-together. Pretty girl. Just a bit... what's the word I'm looking for? *False.* She said all the right things in the right places, but it come off to me like she were acting. Like there were cameras filming her the whole while we were talking, and she were playing up to them, playing this nice-girl-meets-the-mother-in-law character for them, instead of just... being, and letting things happen natural. I expect she were nervous, which you can understand, especially with her being in a foreign country so different from what she were used to. Not exactly Florida, is Dorset. But even so... it were all a bit stagey. A bit... put-on. I didn't say as much to Fred, because he weren't about to listen to me, least of all when he were so smitten and trailing 'round after her like a lovesick puppy, but I remember thinking: you want to watch yourself with that one, my boy. She'll have your guts out someday, and she'll be smiling as she does it."

Nadine's religiosity also came as a surprise to the nominally Christian Bernadette.

"I didn't expect it, no," the latter relates. "We were never church people, me and Jim. Didn't even get Fred baptised in the end. Midnight mass at Christmas and a hot cross bun on Easter Sunday, that were about all we ever bothered with, and Fred never showed much of an interest in any of that, so it weren't as though we were depriving him of something he wanted. And I know, I know: she were American, Nadine were, and everyone knows how carried away *they* get with the bible-thumping. But still. I never would've seen our Fred getting in bed with one of them born-again types. Not until he met her."

Their first meal together, as Bernadette tells it, was an especially uncomfortable affair in this respect.

"Awkward? I'll bloody say it were awkward. I didn't know where to look when she started praying over the garlic bread and giving thanks for the lasagne. Especially when it were *me* who'd cooked it! Then when she started asking me what church I belonged to, and who Fred's pastor were when he were growing up... All I could do were keep nodding at her and smiling until it were over. And I can't say I ever found it that much easier after, being around her. Even once they'd got wed."

Freddie and Nadine married in July of 2007. Not in London, as Bernadette had anticipated they would, but in the Antebellum grandeur of the Sturgess Estate: a former slave plantation in Monroe, Georgia.

Bernadette attended, but was not included in the wedding party.

"I can't say that I minded," she says now. "It were a lot of her people organising it: her mum and her sisters, and the girl who were her maid of honour. All very nice, and I'm sure they tried their best to make me feel at home, but it were just a bit over-whelming. Loud, and... well, like with Nadine, there were a lot of praying. A *lot* of praying. Very religious family, they were — you could see where she got it from, the god-bothering. Even the speech her dad gave at the reception were mostly Bible quotes."

She flew back to the UK the day after the wedding. Freddie and Nadine returned later that month, following a three-week-long honeymoon in Colorado's Rocky Mountains.

By 2008, Nadine was pregnant, giving birth in 2009 to twin boys, Ethan and Ajax. The boys featured prominently in Freddie's YouTube videos in the early years of their lives: blond, blue-eyed and cherubic in matching bow ties and waistcoats, gazing up adoringly at their father from their playroom carpet as he dispensed his wisdom. Having them, Nadine was apt to claim across her own social media accounts, was what prompted her to fully embrace a Tradwife lifestyle centred around homemaking and the raising of children.

The idealised "traditional" family life both Taylors were eager to present to their audiences, however, was not always an accurate reflection of their day-to-day childcare arrangements.

"I had the boys with me most days," Bernadette says. "Fred were making good money by then, so he rented me a little flat in Hampton Wick, close to them in Teddington. It were Nadine who asked me if I'd go and stay up there awhile, while the babbers were little. I can't say as I wanted to move, but they're hard work, twins, and I felt for her. I know how hard it were for me when Fred were young, with Jim out working – that's before the cancer took him – and I only had the one.

"So, I said yes, expecting they'd want me in with them, up in one of the spare rooms... and that were when she told me they'd got it all sorted out already, and Fred had signed a lease on a furnished one-bed that were up there waiting for me whenever I were ready. It were a lot to take in, that, and I do remember telling her I might have to go and have a think about it, because I weren't sure about living on my own in a new place in great big city like that, and in any case there'd be a good few bits and bobs to wrap up before I could pack my whole life up, even if it were just for a few months. And she said she understood, but were any of that more important than being around to see my own grandkids start growing into little people? And, well... I can't say as I had an answer to that. Because it weren't as if she were wrong, were it? Nothing trumps a babba, when you get right down to it."

Duly emotionally blackmailed, Bernadette decamped to

Hampton Wick – where, she tells me, she fell immediately into an almost full-time caregiving role.

"I didn't have them at night. Or... not most nights. But evidently Fred and Nadine had cooked up a schedule between themselves for how it were going to work, and it were all systems go, more or less from the week I moved in: her dropping the little ones off with me at eight-ish in the morning, then picking them up in the evening about six or seven, once her and Fred were finished making their videos and such. Bloody tiring, it were, having the both of them. Especially having to warm up a bottle for one or other of them every hour, on the hour. But they're that gorgeous when they're that age, and that loving, you can't really begrudge them anything, can you?"

Bernadette smiles affectionately as she says this at a recent AI photograph of Ethan and Ajax that hangs on her wall: the twins, now teenagers wearing the uniform of the local private school they attend, beaming toothily back at us like identikit Donny Osmonds.

Though Bernadette has requested that the boys and the details of the lives they now lead be referenced as little as possible in my account of our conversation, she is happy for me to disclose that the pair now live with her, in their father's childhood home – and have done since the murders of their parents in 2016, when they were just six.

This arrangement wasn't reached without difficulty; Nadine's parents made initial—though ultimately unsuc-cessful—efforts to take custody of the boys, with a view to raising them in Orlando. But the current domestic situation of Bernadette and her grandsons seems to me – from the brief observation of their home life dynamics that I'm privy to when, towards the end of my interview with their grand-mother, they tumble loudly in from school – to be a happy one. Despite the devastating loss that scarred their early years, the twins are flourishing now, in Dorset, or so Bernadette tells me with no small amount of pride. And from what I see, I'm inclined to believe her.

I am thrown, however, by Bernadette's allusion to bottle-feeding them as babies. Many of the videos uploaded to Nadine's InTheTradLife YouTube channel, as well as her 2013 "tradwife manual" The Nurturing Kind, make extensive reference to Nadine having breast-fed the twins until they were almost two; they lean heavily, in fact, into a Breast Is Best ethos, with non-breastfeeding mothers tacitly criticised as selfish and unwilling to place the needs of their children above their own discomfort.

"Oh, *that*," Bernadette says, when I raise the issue. "Yeah, I did ask her about that, as it happened. It were just something she said for the videos – *building the brand*, were what her and Fred called it. Making out they were a bit more... *organic* than they were. She never were much interested in breastfeeding, far as I knew. She weren't one of them women who try and try to feed but can't get the babber to latch on, or whose milk never comes in – she just... weren't keen on it. Found it all a bit messy, I reckon. 'Specially with her so eager to get her body back to the way it were, before the births."

Though Nadine and Freddie initially proposed that Bernadette stay in Hampton Wick for "just a few months," it became clear as Ethan and Ajax approached their first birthday that their parents had in mind a more long-term arrangement – reacting with shock, and then outrage when Bernadette suggested returning home to Dorset.

"It weren't that I *wanted* to leave the boys. They were my pride and joy, still are. There's no better reason to get up in the morning when you get to my age than a couple of little ones needing a cuddle. But I didn't want *this* house left empty any longer than it had to be, when I were still paying for the gas and water and electric. You worry, don't you? About break-ins and squatters, about coming back to find someone's let themselves in and changed the locks. I had Marion next door popping in once a week to keep an eye on things and make sure it hadn't been robbed and nothing were going horribly wrong with the boiler, but it weren't the same as *being* here.

"Fred said I ought to just sell it and stick with them in London. Perhaps I should've. Only... I know you're not supposed to let yourself get too attached to houses when they're only bricks and mortar, but I really did love this old place. It were *my* place, when you get right down to it. I didn't want to go giving it away, just like that."

Bernadette found her arguments overridden, however. And so, for fear of antagonising Freddie and Nadine – and in doing so, potentially jeopardising future access to her grandsons – she relented, and agreed to stay on in Hampton Wick.

Until 2016, that is – when Freddie announced that he, Nadine and the boys would soon be moving to a brand-new property, located on a small purpose-built housing estate in Nottinghamshire which, unbeknownst to Bernadette, the couple had been developing (and seeking investment for) over the previous 12 months. It was an estate the Taylors planned to name The Heart of Solomon, in homage to Nadine's Christian faith and Freddie's appreciation for ancient "wisdom."

"I didn't think anyone'd be daft enough to live there, when they told me the point of it – what it were going to be," Bernadette says. "I think I actually said as much, come to that. A whole village just for housewives who stay home with the kiddies whilst their husbands go off to work – what would anybody want with *that*? I was a housewife myself, I said to 'em. You don't need a special place to do it in. You can be one bloody *anywhere*.

"And they laughed at me, just as you might expect. Fred did that sneering voice he put on when he were about to take you down a peg – told me they *appreciated my input*, but they'd done their own research, and they'd have plenty of people lined up wanting a piece of the action, thank you very much. So I thought, *well, sod you, then*. And that were that, so far as I were concerned."

Except it wasn't. Freddie and Nadine, it transpired, expected Bernadette to move with them to the East Midlands... and had pre-emptively secured her a new two-bed rental property to that end, this time in the small Nottinghamshire village of Ruddington.

"I went off at them, that time," she says, glancing up again at the portrait of the twins, now with a look of contrition. "Told them I had my own life back home to look after, and what did they think I were, the hired help? And Nadine..." Bernadette falters, momentarily embarrassed. "She starts crying. *Apologising*. Says how sorry she is she ever come off that way, and how she thinks of me as *her* mum, not just Fred's, and all she wanted were to keep me close so's the boys could have the kind of relationship with their nan that she, Nadine, wished *she* could have with *her* mum, if her mum weren't so far away. And that now Fred's doing well for himself, he's wanting to take care of his old mum the same way I took care of him when he were little. That were what the house were, she says. Fred's way of saying thank you."

*Sounds as if Nadine laid it on a bit thick*, I suggest.

"Maybe." That same embarrassed expression crosses

Bernadette's face again. "Worked, though, didn't it? Once she'd said all that... all's I could do were say how sorry *I* were for getting it wrong, for misunderstanding what they were trying to do for me and the little ones. And that I'd move up there with 'em, if that were still what they wanted. 'Course I would."

Entrusting care of the Dorset bungalow to her neighbour, Bernadette moved with Freddie and Nadine to Nottinghamshire – where, as per their prior arrangement, she provided childcare for the twins during daytime hours, while their parents grew and consolidated their #Tradlife empire.

This arrangement, Bernadette explains, continued even after Ethan and Ajax entered primary school. Often, she would pick them up at the school gates at home-time; cook them dinner; bathe and change them into pyjamas in her own bathroom, and then drive them back to the Heart of Solomon in the evening so that Nadine could put them to bed. Since Freddie and Nadine enjoyed entertaining guests most Saturday nights, the twins would often also stay at Bernadette's from Friday to Sunday – a setup that was, Bernadette says, "tiring, but worth it. Fred and their mum were so busy. Always distracted, always with their heads in some project or other and their noses glued to their phones, trying to take pictures for the internet and what have you. So, it were nice to be able to give the little ones some proper attention."

It also meant that, on the night of the murders, the twins were safely ensconced in Ruddington with Bernadette – several miles away from the Heart of Solomon.

"I go over that a lot in my head," Bernadette tells me. "About what might've happened if the little ones had been in that house with Fred and their mum, instead of with me.

And it chills me to the bloody bone, just thinking about it. 'Cause it could've been so different, couldn't it? Could've worked out so, so different. I'm just grateful..." She hesitates again; throws one final glance up at the school portrait on the wall. "I'm just grateful they're safe. They're here with me now, and they're safe."

# NADINE

It's possible, we might conclude from Bernadette's observations of her son's early beliefs and behaviours, that Freddie Taylor nurtured ambitions of establishing a Trad enclave in the UK – a proto-Heart of Solomon – long before he met and married Nadine Halliday.

What's clear from Bernadette's testimony, however – and from the vast archive of videos, photographs, blog entries, books, articles and written manifestos left behind by the Taylors across their many websites, social media accounts and broadcast channels – is that his marriage to Nadine galvanised Freddie into action: transforming whatever traditionalist-entrepreneurial pipedreams he may have harboured previously into a clearly-defined vision. A blueprint and a business plan, requiring only an injection of capital to bring it into being in the physical world.

The first round of crowdfunding for the Heart of Solomon development began in 2012 – long before Bernadette, or indeed many in the wider world, were aware of what the Taylors had in mind for the plot of Nottinghamshire farmland Freddie had surreptitiously purchased in late 2008, using profits derived from subscriptions to his Raw Meat site, the monetisation of his YouTube channel, and the sales of his first (unexpectedly successful) self-published e-book, *Make It Yours, Take It Now*. In the video created by the couple for the fundraiser's launch on the (now defunct) Subsidize Me! platform, Freddie – hand-in-hand with his wife, the pair of them smiling winsomely at the camera – describes Nadine as "the heart of the Heart of Solomon venture. The woman behind the man. The woman who gave this whole thing wings."

Without her, he stresses repeatedly, there would *be* no Heart of Solomon.

But who *was* she, this woman now most commonly remembered not for her business nous, nor even the appalling ideologies she espoused, but for the circumstances of her murder – the scalping of her famously blonde hair, the removal of her blood-red fingernails and the extraction of her perfectly white teeth at the moment of her death? What was she like, before her marriage to Freddie?

How, moreover (and perhaps this is the real $64,000 Question) does *any* woman come to not just advocate for, but design and oversee the construction of an environment intended to facilitate her own disempowerment and dependence, not to mention the disempowerment and dependence of other women like her?

No-one close to Nadine was prepared to speak to me when I reached out to them: not her parents, nor her sisters, nor the college friend who served as her maid of honour. Her father, in fact, went so far as to threaten me and my publisher with legal action on discovering the purpose of my enquiry, and the headline details of the book I intended to write.

Nadine, however, was a self-styled public figure – and

thus, we're able to piece together at least some picture of who she was from those personal details she disclosed herself in the public domain, and from those which were made public by others (not least Resist Magazine's Raine Hudson) in the aftermath of the murders.

To begin at the beginning, then:

Nadine Halliday was born in Orlando, Florida in March 1983, the second daughter of homemaker Marlene and Gilbert 'Gator' Halliday – founder and CEO of the state-wide Gator Eaters restaurant chain. Raised Southern Baptist in the congregation of Orlando's Tangier Street Church, where her father served as a lay pastor and her mother as a Sunday school teacher, Nadine attended elementary, middle and high school in the affluent suburb of Bougainvillea Gardens (average household income: $135,000 per year). She captained the Park Trammell High cheerleading squad and graduated second in her class in 2001, with a near-perfect 3.9 Grade Point Average.[1]

Aged 17, she progressed from Park Trammel to the Baptist-affiliated Sovereign College: an evangelical university in Fenwick, South Carolina, founded in the early 1970s by activist-televangelist couple Steve and Estelle Lamont. Sovereign is best known today for its high-profile and outspokenly Christian alumni body – among them Republican Senator CJ Weems, country musician Josh Chalmers and controversy courting American football player Todd Baker.

Sovereign's Honor Code, oft-reproduced by scandalised

---

1. Helen – will anyone in the UK know what the hell this means, in practical terms? I had to google it. But then, I still struggle to get my head around the way they grade A Levels now, so I might not be a good barometer! – G.

sections of the US left-leaning media, famously prohibits its students from engaging in premarital sex, alcohol consumption, same-sex relationships and "unbiblical conduct," including the use of "cross-sex pronouns." "Modest dress" is also required of men and women, in the classroom and beyond. Any violation of the Sovereign Code exposes students to sanctions ranging from monetary fines (of up to $100), to temporary suspension and permanent expulsion. Undercover reporting from student journalists indicates that the university continues (as of 2023) to practice "conversion therapy" on LGBTQ-identifying members of its community, under the auspices of its wider "pastoral care" program.

Sovereign, then, takes its religion seriously. And so too, while she studied there, did Nadine – chairing both the Scripture Society ("guiding you through scriptural precepts in the company of like-minded peers") and the Life Affirmers, an anti-abortion student club dedicated to co-ordinating protests and "establishing a loving presence" outside sexual and reproductive health clinics across South Carolina.

On graduating from Sovereign with a degree in Business Administration, she returned home to Orlando where, at her father's behest, she began managing the Winter Park branch of Gator Eaters during the week, and teaching Sunday school at Tangier Street alongside her mother at weekends. It was around this time that she began to develop the online "trad" persona that would eventually become her brand and trademark: curating social media profiles that foregrounded her interests in cooking, baking, textiles, home-organising, food-growing and gardening, as well as her religious faith and concomitant endorsement of a range of "pro-life," anti-LGBTQ+ and antifeminist causes.

A self-professed virgin, Nadine had committed at age 16 to the so-called "purity pledge" popularised in the mid-1990s via evangelical minister Denny Pattyn's Silver Ring Thing program. She was, as her socials circa 2004 indicated, "waiting for the right man to sweep [her] off [her] feet."

And apparently, in Freddie Taylor, she found him.

The day-to-day particulars of the Taylors' marriage remain somewhat opaque, beyond those accounts delivered by Nadine and Freddie themselves in the myriad media material they created between their engagement and their deaths. If we're to believe Freddie's characterisation of his wife as the driving force behind the Heart of Solomon enterprise, however, we might also wonder *how* she brought the community into being... and how, precisely, she was able to help Freddie secure the funding necessary to subsidise and market the construction of those fifteen brand-new cottages that would house the Heart of Solomon's residents.

Let's skip back, therefore, to the Taylors' crowdfunding efforts, the details of which may shed at least some light on this question. The objections raised in response to this crowdfunding activity may also prove illuminating for our purposes.

At the time the Heart of Solomon proposition was first mooted on Raw Meat, it faced - as one might expect - a barrage of backlash, as well as widespread accusations of misogyny, from the full range of left-wing and centrist media and cultural commentators.

What's less well known, though, is the reputational hit the project suffered later in the process from those who had initially endorsed it – including its early financial backers, some of whom felt their donations and investments had not been put to the uses they'd hoped. That Freddie and Nadine had, to put it bluntly, misappropriated a percentage of the money they'd been given.

SABRINA GONZALEZ

"Oh, for sure they got death threats after the Heart of Solomon launch. Most of them online, and Freddie was pretty public about those on Twitter, as I recall. Very *woe is me, I'm just a poor misunderstood little white boy trying to do what's right* – you know the drill. I don't take those especially seriously, and I'm not sure he and Nadine did either. But the vandalism, the break-ins at the house and all the other stuff the Taylors took to the cops but didn't want going public in case it scared off the investors... *those* I'm interested in. And we never did find out for sure who was behind them."

This is Sabrina Gonzalez, a social anthropologist whose work explores the connection between the US religious right and the growing problem of misogyny here in the UK, addressing the animosity Freddie and Nadine faced – from opponents of the Tradwife and wider "trad" movements, and, as we'll see, those a little closer to home – in the early days of the Heart of Solomon project.

Sabrina is perhaps the closest thing we have to an expert on the Heart of Solomon. Not regarding the murders per se, but rather concerning the development of the site, and the provenance of the money poured into it as a stronghold of "traditionalist" values. These values she sees as imported (in part) from the States via a kind of "astroturfing": a process by which the true, usually wealthy and influential, external sponsors of a movement or organisation conceal themselves behind local figureheads, in order to frame that movement or organisation as grassroots and organically occurring.

"At least some of the Solomon money came from this evangelical think-tank in [Washington] D.C., the Hobart Trust," Sabrina tells me, her Southern Californian vowels noticeably sharpening as she spits out the latter name. "Not too many people know them here, but they're worthy of scrutiny. If you're queer or a woman or you care about bodily autonomy and reproductive rights... some of the policies they lobby for are downright terrifying."

I should at this point disclose that Sabrina, unlike the other subjects I've met with and interviewed, is not a stranger to me; in fact, she and I have known one another for many years. I'm lucky to count her as a close friend as well as a colleague, and we've collaborated many times on journal articles, research council-funded projects and, most recently, the upcoming essay collection *Redefining Life & Liberty: Feminist Perspectives On New Global Challenges To Reproductive Health.*[1] I'm able therefore speak first-hand to her experience and credibility; if anyone can trace the flow of money back from the Heart of Solomon estate to its donor base, it's Sabrina.[2]

---

1.  Gonzalez, S. and Lewis, G. (2024) *Redefining Life & Liberty: Feminist Perspectives on New Global Challenges To Reproductive Health.* London: Glenfield University Press.
2.  Helen – it feels counterproductive to mention S. and I were briefly

"Sure, there were contributions from individuals," she says, of the Taylors' Subsidize Me! campaign. "Pledges from British guys – and it mostly *was* guys, of course – who gobbled up what Freddie was telling them about going back to the '50s, and who wanted a piece of the action. From MRAs [Men's Rights Activists] who wanted women to suffer, period, and didn't mind emptying their pockets to do it. And from some of the fanboys who'd migrated over from Raw Meat and figured Freddie for a Plato trying to make himself a trad Republic. But it was small potatoes, mostly – we're talking £50 here, £100 there. I mean, okay, it all added up. But were those £50 pledges enough to build a village-worth of rustic cottages out of nothing but a patch of soil? I don't think so.

"The *real* money, the big money, that came from the Hobart Trust, behind the curtain. And from another name you might have heard of: Family Matters Media."

Sabrina is being not a little facetious here: I am, as she knows, all too familiar with Family Matters Media, on whose lobbying activities in Washington both of us have written extensively. Like the Hobart Trust, FMM is both evangelically Christian in inclination and fundamentally anti-equality in practice, and has been since its inception in the mid-1980s – campaigning for and donating heavily to a host of (typically Republican) Presidential, Senate and downticket candidates whose critical views of same-sex marriage and adoption, trans rights, abortion access, contraception and gender parity align with their own. Its annual revenue, as of 2022, exceeded $10,000,000 USD.

But why, I ask her, would these big beasts of the US reli-

---

married, back in the day. Do I need to put it in here, in the interests of transparency? Or is it TMI? - G.

right want to subsidise a comparatively small British alt-right player like Freddie Taylor, who held no sway at all over the *American* cultural and political landscape? What was in it for them?

And how would he even have landed on their radar in the first place?

That, Sabrina says, is where Nadine came in.

"You know who she roomed with in college, at Sovereign? A kid called Keeley Chambers. Real besties, those two. Nadine was bridesmaid at Keeley's wedding; a couple years later, Keeley does the honours for Nadine when *she* marries Freddie. And you know who Keeley's dad is? Brian Chambers. The *Reverend* Brian Chambers, President of Family Matters Media."

I recall Bernadette Taylor's mention of Nadine's best friend – the very nice, very religious girl she met in Orlando. Then I try to reconcile that image with what I know of the Reverend Chambers: a Mississippi firebrand whose decades-long battle with "the homosexual movement" has seen FMM fight the introduction of pro-LGBT+ legislation from New York to California, and whose religious beliefs inspired the organisation's position on "traditional family values."

"There's more," Sabrina adds. "Keeley's godfather? Jan Keppler. CFO of The Hobart Trust. So, it's probably not a stretch to say that Nadine most likely talked to Keeley about her clever English husband's idea for a Tradwife Jonestown, and Keeley put the word out to Daddy and Uncle Jan... and *that's* how the money started flowing into Solomon. At first, anyways. Until Simon Baxter waded in, and I think we both know how *that* went."

Indeed, we do – as do most of us who followed the

Heart of Solomon story in the British press, both before and after the murders.

Simon Baxter – Brexit Baxter, as the Express once dubbed him – was at one time the largest British donor to the Heart of Solomon project on record: funnelling over £50,000 of his own money into Freddie's fundraising campaign prior to the beginning of construction work on the Nottinghamshire site. He's also widely considered, by the Reddit true-crime commentariat as well as Raine Hudson and several other of the journalists who've covered the Taylor, Wilson and Cooper murders, to be one of the prime suspects in the break-ins and vandalism that plagued the Heart of Solomon, and the Taylors' property especially, in its early days. Acts of retribution, or so Hudson posits, for the financial wrongs Baxter felt Freddie to have personally done him following Baxter's donation to the community and the wider Tradwife cause.

"I wouldn't put it past him, not at all," Sabrina says, of Baxter's culpability. "He's a petty guy. Skin paper-thin. He sued his own lawyer once for defamation, if you can believe it. So, yeah, I don't have a hard time picturing him retaliating. Breaking into Freddie Taylor's house to put the willies up him or calling in some hired muscle to get it done."

Baxter, for those few who may not have heard of him, is the founder and chairman of multinational brewery and pub chain Jemmick's. Currently he sits at number 315 on the Sunday Times Rich List, with an estimated net worth of £420m. He is an OBE recipient (New Year Honours 2011) and was – as his nickname indicates – one of the business world's most ardent supporters of the Vote Leave campaign ahead of the UK's 2016 Brexit referendum, donating upwards of £180,000 of his own money to the cause. A staunch social and fiscal conservative, Baxter has a long record of endorsing traditionalist activism, with prior donations funnelled to organisations including advocacy group Christian Interest (which opposes "secular liberalism and liberal humanism" in all its forms) and the pseudo-political party Moral Law, which – inspired by Vladimir Putin's introduction and expansion of "gay propaganda" legislation in Russia in 2013 and 2022 – seeks to "criminalise the promotion of homosexuality in our media, schools and public institutions."

Like the Hobart Trust and Family Matters Media, Baxter threw his weight, and his not inconsiderable financial clout, behind the Heart of Solomon project early on in its development.

"He *loved* Freddie," Sabrina tells me. "Loved the Tradwife thing, loved the idea of Solomon. All of it was totally *him*, right? Traditional family values, women in the kitchen, everyone pure and white and godly... Freddie's manifesto for the place reads like Baxter's wet dream. So *obviously*, as soon as he heard about it, it was all Brexit Boy could talk about – in interviews, on Twitter, wherever. He called it... what was it? *A beacon of hope in a degenerate world.*"

She mutters here a string of pejoratives that, mindful of Baxter's litigious disposition, I will refrain from reproducing.

"He pledged £10,000 upfront, publicly, on the Solomon Subsidize Me! page," she continues thereafter. "But we think there was probably more: other lump sums, sent directly from Baxter to Freddie. Baxter wasn't shy about alluding to what he'd given. Or what he was willing to give in the longer term, as the project progressed."

Posts still available on Baxter's personal social media accounts seem to corroborate this supposition. In one series of tweets, issued in response to a Twitter user's question about the Subsidize Me! donation, Baxter writes: "That's not the half of it mate! Freds a great bloke, has some v. solid ideas & brilliant plans 4 future. Proud 2 say theres another big cheque here in front of me w/ his name on it. And more 2 come!"

In a 2013 video live chat with Human Capital magazine – still available to watch on YouTube – he brags of having given Freddie "more money than he knows what to do with" for the Heart of Solomon development. Interviews with the Times and The Scotsman that same year see him repeat the claim... and add, in the latter piece, that Freddie would have "[his] support, and [his] wallet, just as long as he needs it. You don't want to put limits on the pursuit of good works, do you?"

Of course, as Sabrina indicates, a desire to subsidise "good works" was far from Baxter's *sole* rationale for directing money into Freddie's pocket. As was widely reported in the UK press following the murders, and as Raine Hudson has since established in his own exhaustive investigations, Baxter intended not only to act as the Taylors' patron, but to relocate with his wife and three teenage children *to* the Heart of Solomon – and to live there not as a renter (with the Taylors as his landlord), but as a property owner. That is: he expected that, in recognition of his generosity, Freddie would gift him both a newly built cottage and the plot of land it occupied, and would welcome him into the community fold with open arms. What developer, Baxter reasoned, *wouldn't* be utterly delighted at the prospect of a high-profile multimillionaire moving into his concept development – especially a regional development like Freddie's, comparatively modest by the standards of Baxter's Kensington mansion, his Manhattan townhouse and his castle in the Highlands? And how better to raise the

Heart of Solomon's profile, to generate some hot – if not necessarily exclusively *good* – PR for the project?

The plan was, as Baxter phrased it in a string of text messages to his accountant, leaked to the Guardian in 2019, "a stroke of genius. A win-win for everyone."

Freddie disagreed.

"He didn't want the attention," Sabrina says. "Not *that* kind of attention, anyways. And he didn't want to share. Freddie was a loudmouth and a peacock – we all know he loved the spotlight – but he liked to do things on his own terms. Didn't like to share, didn't like anyone telling him what to do. So, a guy like Baxter – a guy that rich, that powerful – moving onto his patch, making demands and acting like he was doing Freddie a favour just by being there? No. *Not* what Freddie wanted. I assume he liked the money Baxter threw at him, the same way he liked cashing cheques from FMM and Hobart. But he liked it from a distance, not close-up. He wanted the funds, but he didn't want to share the glory. Solomon was *his* baby; no-one else's."

Quite how Freddie framed his rebuttal of Baxter's "offer" to move on-site, we can only speculate. Baxter's reaction to the rejection, however – and to what he surely perceived as gross ingratitude on Freddie's part – is a matter of public record.

"He filed suit," Sabrina says. "He did it quietly, by Baxter's standard – the story got buried at the time, I guess because he didn't want too many people knowing he'd been knocked back. There's not much out there *now* about it, even if you go looking, so I'm guessing he took out an injunction, got a gag order in place. But he filed, we know that. His lawyers called it breach of verbal contract; said Freddie had promised Baxter the house and the land and a place at

Solomon, and that he'd solicited donations in exchange for all of that. It wasn't true, obviously: there was a paper trail a mile long saying otherwise, a bunch of time-stamped texts and emails from Freddie to Nadine and some other people showing just how surprised Freddie was that Baxter had sprung it all on him, and how much he *didn't* want and *would never* have wanted it to happen.

"It was thrown out by the judge pretty fast. Probably wouldn't have made it to court at all if the plaintiff had been anyone but Baxter. But it was... let's be diplomatic and say *acrimonious*. Baxter did *not* hold back on the accusations. He called Freddie a liar, a cheat, a fraud; said he wouldn't let Freddie get away with what he'd done, and that there'd be consequences. Which doesn't sound so great *now*, does?"

As might perhaps be expected, given these outbursts and accusations, the dismissal of the court case was far from the last of Baxter's attempts to get even with the Taylors. Or so rumour has it.

Sabrina, understandably, is reticent to go into much detail, when I bring up the specifics of what Baxter is alleged to have done next.[3]

"If you were asking, do I think – on the balance of the available evidence – that Baxter might be capable of taking

---

3. Helen – do we need to cite sources here? Because half of mine are anonymous, the sort of people you come across when you start lurking on online true crime forums! And the other half are... well, folks who really wouldn't appreciate me dropping their names into the mix in this particular instance. Sabrina's right: Baxter is an absolute bastard for getting the lawyers involved. He'd sue us all at the drop of a hat – even writing this chapter feels a bit risky, to be honest. He's gunning for poor Raine Hudson even as we speak, and the kid hasn't got a pot to piss in. But then again: if all this stuff is in the public domain, surely we're allowed to report and comment on it? You'd know better than I would, I suppose. Let's talk when I've got a final draft together? – G.

the law into his own hands? Then I'd answer that, in my opinion, and it's *just* that, an opinion: yes. It seems to me that he might be. But if you were asking, did he *actually* do those things? I'd tell you, I don't know. And it might be better for everyone if I don't speculate."

The details of *those things*, however – the break-ins at the Taylor residence, and the repeated acts of vandalism in which Baxter may or may not have had a hand – are not in dispute.

Crime reports filed by the Taylors between 2016 and 2017 – and uncovered by the Sun in 2019, around the same time as the Guardian unleashed the Baxter texts onto its readership – outline six separate incidents of malicious mischief, criminal damage and burglary committed on and around the Heart of Solomon site in that same 12-month period. Encountering the reports of these incidents now, from a distance of more than half a decade, it's difficult *not* to infer that the perpetrator bore a grudge against the Heart of Solomon project, and Freddie and Nadine in particular. We might even say that the incidents were explicitly intended to *scare* the Taylors; to terrorise them on their home turf, perhaps with a view to driving them out of it.

They were, to put it mildly, extremely odd, and odder still in light of the violence that followed.

On the 27th of April 2016, according to the first of the crime reports, the Taylors found on their doorstep a raw and bleeding pig's heart, held together loosely with baking paper. Less than a month later, they were woken in the night by the sound of breaking glass – discovering, on venturing downstairs, that a brick had been hurled through their living room window. Tied to the brick with a length of string was a naked Barbie doll, its plastic skin and long blonde hair stained with a blood-like substance subsequently identified as red food colouring.

There followed, in July, September and October of the same year, three separate acts of early-hours vandalism to the front door and exterior walls of the Taylor home. In each instance, the words "traitor" and "liar" had been sprayed in red block-capitals across the wood and brickwork of their cottage.

The final, and perhaps most disturbing incident occurred in January 2017, soon after Christmas, when a slim parcel – swaddled in festive wrapping – was pushed through the Taylors' letterbox as they were sitting down to dinner.

Inside the parcel was a complete set of adult human teeth, their provenance still unknown to this day, and a quote from Corinthians 6:13, torn from the pages of a King James Bible. The quotation reads:

*Meats for the belly, and the belly for meats: but God shall destroy both it and them.*

Neither Simon Baxter nor Freddie's once-close friend George Gorecki – who may also, we might speculate, have had reason to brand the Taylors "traitors," and whose history of violent retribution is well known – were held or questioned at the time about their possible involvement. Only in 2019, immediately after the murders, was Baxter interviewed by police in relation to the 2016-17 crimes – though he was, as Raine Hudson reported and Baxter's own solicitor corroborated in a public statement thereafter, released without so much as a caution.

It should be noted moreover, if only in the interests of balance, that Baxter and Gorecki were not the only former acquaintances of the Taylors to whom the prospect of retribution might have appealed. Indeed, accusations of financial malfeasance, if not quite on the scale of that alleged by Baxter, dogged Freddie especially throughout the short life of the Heart of Solomon project.

"Some of the campaign contributors, the ones who got on Subsidize Me! and the ones who donated through Freddie's website... they got a little pissed when they saw how he'd been spending their money," Sabrina says. "They weren't like Baxter – they weren't planning on actually living at Solomon themselves, necessarily. But they'd invested in the whole idea of it being a *community*, right? And even for people like that, people who want their women to stay home and keep house and the coloured folks to stay off their lawn, you get this little kernel of a yearning for something like egalitarianism peeking through. Egalitarianism within some very finite parameters, sure – the way they'd see it, they're not obligated to treat, say, *us* equally, because as far as they're concerned, we're not really people the same way they are. But still a sense that dudes *like them* deserve to not get screwed over. That *they* at least oughta be given a level playing field.

"Or maybe it's something to do with most of them being British. That whole *fair play* thing you all tell yourselves you're into. They were mostly British guys on the websites, I think – British guys, sending in their fifties and hundreds and striking a blow for hard-done-by white men everywhere.

"Anyhow, they *really* didn't like what they saw when the construction crews and decorators finished up those first dozen cottages and Nadine started posting photos of her and Freddie's new love nest on Instagram. Because the contrast between *their* place and the other cottages... I mean, you've seen the pictures, right? You must know what I'm talking about."

I have, and I do. Nadine's personal accounts may no longer be active, but it's not difficult to track down the posts, and the images, to which Sabrina refers. Nor is it tough to find photos of the other Heart of Solomon cottages and *their* interiors from around the time of the community's launch… not least because they featured so heavily in the digital brochures the Taylors' PR team produced ahead *of* that launch.

The contrast between the two couldn't be starker. Where inside, the Taylors' property is large, spacious and kitted-out with Gaggenau white goods and every luxury appliance one can imagine, the other cottages are smaller and pokier, their decor and furnishings more Argos than Harrods. Light saturates the Taylors' home through high, strategically positioned bay windows; neighbouring residences conversely are bathed in shadow, despite the best composition efforts of the PR agency's photographer.

One set of images calls to mind any handful of the thousands upon thousands of affordable family rentals advertised on RightMove for a low monthly rate and minimal deposit. The other suggests an idyllic farmhouse conversion as imagined by a City stockbroker retiring to the countryside – or, worse, the pleasure-palace of an unscrupulous landlord grown fat on the exploitation of his tenants.

Great emphasis had been placed throughout Freddie's fundraising campaign on the altruistic and philanthropic aims of the Heart of Solomon; that the community would be, and was intended to be, the flagship project of a larger social movement.

In Freddie's own words:

"We're not doing this for ourselves. The money we've made already, what we've got tucked away… we could stop all this tomorrow, go away and live in the lap of luxury somewhere, and never make a peep about our faith and the things we believe. But we don't want to. Money, materialism... they don't interest us. They're not important to us.

"What we care about is family: yours, as well as ours. We want to live in a world where traditional values are respected, where "wife" and "mother" aren't dirty words and we're not forced to explain at every turn why men and women having different and complementary roles is actually a good thing, a healthy thing. And that world might not exist at the moment... but we want to try to build it, for all of us.

"The Heart of Solomon... it isn't about us. It isn't even really *for* us. It's for you."

The photos, though, tell a different story: the story of an already wealthy couple who elected to enrich themselves further at the expense of their neighbours, and through the monetary contributions of strangers who thought they were supporting an ideology and a cause, instead of one man's bank balance.

"Some of the guys who donated started a Facebook group about it," Sabrina continues. "A public group. You've probably seen that too? They called it *Where's The Money, Freddie?* – which I have to say, I kind of like. It was a place to vent, I guess. But also, a place to ask some of the questions everyone involved in the fundraising gig must've been dying to put to Taylor. You know: "how much did you spend on each property?" and "how was the money for each cottage allocated?" and "do you think we can't *see* you've been lining your own pockets?" All of that.

"And they got removed by the moderators pretty quickly... but there were death threats there, too. A few I saw for myself. Anonymous ones, obviously."

*What sort of threats?* I ask.

"Oh, just what you'd expect. *You'll get yours, you selfish bastard*, variations on that theme. One of them I found interesting, though. And I don't want to tell anyone how to do their job... but if I were the cops, I'd want to look a little more closely at *that* one than the others."

*What did it say?*

"Funny thing... it wasn't a direct threat, exactly. It was two more Bible quotes – a mashup, actually. From Exodus and Thessalonians.

"*If the thief is caught while breaking in and is struck so that he dies, there will be no bloodguiltiness on his account. For you yourself know full well that the day of the Lord will come like a thief in the night.*"

# VICTIMS 5 & 6: BRENDAN & REBECCA COOPER

# BRENDAN & BECKY

We've spent time, perhaps *more* time than we'd otherwise like, getting to know the Wilsons and the Taylors. But what about the third and final couple murdered at the dinner table that night in 2019? What of the Coopers?

Many of us are now very familiar with the details of Brendan Cooper's sexual proclivities and the predatory criminal behaviours they engendered. Likewise, those who've followed the Heart of Solomon case these last few years will know something of *Becky* Cooper's sexual and romantic history – in particular her prior relationship with Shannon Delaney, the police's original (and I must stress again, now fully exonerated) prime suspect.

Often, though, that is all we know.

It may be useful therefore for us to begin not at the beginning of the Coopers' stories, but at the end – and from there, for us to work our way back to the histories and experiences that made them who they were, and that ultimately brought them to that dinner table.

Brendan and Becky Cooper were not only the last family to join the Heart of Solomon community, but were some of its youngest residents: at the time of their deaths, Becky was just 26, and Brendan only slightly older, at 29.

They were also, indisputably, troubled. Before embracing "traditional" marriage and entering Solomon, both had struggled with alcohol dependence, cocaine addiction and bouts of severe depression. Both had spent time, separately, in residential detox and mental health facilities. Indeed, they met – despite press speculation to the contrary – not in Alcoholics Anonymous but rather, as Paula Deal concludes in her profile of the pair, through a mutual friend, convicted MDMA dealer Caspar Sandhu.[1]

Becky – born Rebecca Willingham – hailed from Bacup, Lancashire. The fourth and last child of social workers Paul and Frances Willingham, she was orphaned at five years old following a car accident that claimed the lives of both her parents, and was subsequently raised, along with her older siblings, by her maternal aunt Zara and Zara's partner Chris Denning, in the well-to-do Greater Manchester suburb of Didsbury.

At school, Paula Deal reports, Becky was behaviourally challenging: prone to violent outbursts and given to unprovoked physical attacks on other children, and occasionally on teaching staff. Aged 11, she'd been suspended from her local Church of England primary for throwing a chair across a classroom at her Head of Year, and by 13 had been permanently excluded from Cheadle's Patrick Moore Academy. Thereafter, she was home-schooled, principally by the then-unemployed Denning.

Though it's impossible to know for certain when her serious drug use began, we know that by her mid-teens, Becky had already begun to rack up cautions, and then

_____________________

1.   Deal, P. *The Keepers of Wives*, pp142-3

noncustodial criminal convictions, for shoplifting and possession of cocaine, amphetamines and ketamine. Eventually, *possession* became *possession with intent to supply* – resulting in her 18-month detainment, from March 2008, in HM Young Offenders Institution Willoughby.

It was at Willoughby that she first met Shannon Delaney, the woman who would eventually become her partner.

Becky's relationship with Shannon has cast a strange pall over public understandings and media-cultural constructions of the Heart of Solomon murders. Shannon herself has come to represent very different things to interested commentators, depending on their own political and ideological orientations: ridiculed and demonised by those on the right; and mourned by the left as a kind of queer, working-class sacrificial lamb, offered up to sate the ghoulish appetites of a snobbish, homophobic British public.

The reality of her, I suspect, is a far cry from both these two-dimensional depictions. And I'm pleased, having been given the chance to speak with her directly, to get to know something of the real Shannon: the human being behind the headlines.

## SHANNON DELANEY

Inasmuch as such a thing is possible under the circumstances, Shannon Delaney seems to have moved on from Becky Cooper.

It's been more than 15 years since the two first met in the cells of HMYOI Willoughby – but still, I find it hard to reconcile the emaciated, mephedrone-addled teenager convicted in 2008 of attempted murder and knife possession with the smiling, healthy-looking woman with the personal trainer physique who greets me in the lobby of her East London apartment building.

Present-day Shannon Delaney is confident, articulate, charismatic and unapologetically butch. She's also, though I'm no expert, unusually dapper: her bowtie and pocket handkerchief, and the clean lines of her charcoal suit suggestive of a fashion-literate good taste to which most of us can only aspire.[1]

---

1.  Between us, she'd have been just my type ten years ago. Jags' too, probably. Though I'm not sure either of us have the patience to pick out a new waistcoat and cravat combination every morning these days – G.

"That'll be the day job," she laughs when I mention this, her Bolton accent as strong as ever in spite of her present location. "You have to make yourself presentable, or no-one trusts you to make *them* look decent. A tailor in a cheap suit is like a dentist with bad teeth."

For the last nine months, she tells me, she's worked at an independent atelier on Savile Row, specialising in bespoke shirt- and trouser-making for a client base of City traders, hedge fund managers and tech industry wunderkinds. Before joining her present employer – who "stole" her, she tells me with another self-effacing chuckle, from a rival firm on Cork Street – she completed a three-year adult apprenticeship in textiles, tailoring and pattern-cutting; she hopes, in the future, to achieve Master Tailor recognition, and perhaps even open a boutique store of her own.

"I've been lucky," she admits, once she's led me into her swatch-filled living room/kitchen and settled me on the sofa with a cup of green tea. "Very fucking lucky. I say this all the time, and it sounds melodramatic as fuck, but it saved my life, finding tailoring. I was in a bad way when the job centre put me on the diploma course that got me the apprenticeship – right fucked up. Emotionally, not just because of the gear. I'd had..." She pauses. "It was rough. A rough time. But then I started on the course, started playing around with the fabrics, the designing and cutting, and it was like a lightbulb going off in my head. All I wanted to do after that was go and live in the studio with the mannequins, so I could lose myself in making stuff. Thank God it turned out I was good at it, too. Would've been embarrassing for everyone if I'd been shit and still begging them to let me stay on."

She laughs again. It's terribly endearing.

I can't help but feel, however, that *a rough time* might be the understatement of the year. In the winter of 2019, Shannon – then just beginning the process of learning her trade, and still struggling with the emotional baggage to which she alludes – was best known to the public as *Becky Cooper's stalker*. The girl whose harassment of the Coopers before their induction into the Heart of Solomon community saw her detained and extensively questioned by police as a possible suspect in their murders.

The subsequent media scrutiny to which she was subject was intense, unremitting and brutal, with much of the coverage of her detention leaning towards full-blown character assassination. LESBIAN EX IN SLAUGHTER ARREST, screamed one headline; DRUGGIE LOVER "COULDN'T LET GO," suggested another; TRADWIFE BECKY "LIVED IN FEAR" OF CRAZED DELANEY, pronounced a third.[2] Almost every story came accompanied by a mugshot-style photograph of Shannon, not as she looked at the time, but as she had looked in her YOI Willoughby days: sickly-pale and sullen, her mouth twisted into a Myra Hindley-esque sneer.

"I think I probably deserved the pasting," she says, when I tentatively mention her treatment at the hands of the UK press – though, having recently revisited archived coverage of the case in the 2019-20 period, I'm not sure I agree. "Some of what I got called wasn't brilliant, especially the threats and the shit I got online. I ended up having to shut down my Facebook and Instagram to keep a lid on it, and I still can't bring myself to look at what people were saying on

---

2.   Helen – do we have to name names of titles here? I know it's all public record, but some of the red-tops have been very prickly about this since Alex O'Neill's documentary came out, and I don't want to land us in any hot water – G.

Twitter. I *was* a twat to Becky, and I know I must've scared her with what I did... so I need to own that. I'm not some poor little innocent who got caught in the crossfire of something. I *did* some of the stuff they said."

*Which was what?* I ask her. I've combed through the media reports; pored over Paula Deal's profile of the girl; read as many of the social media accusations, lurid and otherwise, as I could stomach. But I'm keen to hear the story from Shannon herself. To have her confirm what I think I already know.

"I hounded her, Becky. Hassled her and that, after she dumped me for Brendan. Phoning and texting her, a *lot* – I'm actually surprised she didn't block me or change her number. And I *did* go round to their house a few times after they got married, shouting and banging on the door until they let me in. The one they had in Colney Heath, not that Nottingham place they moved to," she adds quickly, defensive for the first time in our conversation. "I never once set foot in *that* fascist shithole, whatever anyone said. I haven't even got a car. What did they think I did, get the train up to the Midlands from St Pancras every Tuesday and Thursday, so I could stand outside their window howling at the fucking moon?"

There's a lot to unpack, if we're to understand the complexities of the Shannon/Becky/Brendan dynamic... and what drove Shannon to behave as she did towards her ex-partner.

So, let's go back a bit: to 2008, and the girls' initial meeting inside YOI Willoughby.

"She was beautiful, so beautiful," Shannon says, recalling that period – with unexpected nostalgia, or so it seems to me. "We were both kids, and both properly fucked up, but I remember the first time I saw her in the mess hall, strutting up to the table I was sat at with those cheekbones and this long blonde hair like she was walking a catwalk, and I'm telling you, it was like being struck by a bolt of fucking lightning. I couldn't even *speak*. If we'd been in a film, I'd have rolled off my chair and had a tray of food come crashing down on my head. That's the effect she had on me. I don't want to say I was bewitched, because everything I did later on, I *did*, yeah? I'm not... I don't want to be shifting the blame. But being around Becky, it was like being under a spell, even before she'd really said anything or done anything that, if I'm thinking logically, should've made me feel that way. She was... I don't know, magnetic? I've met a few actors and stuff at work, when they've come in to get fitted, and you get a similar sort of vibe with the *really* big names. They shine a little bit brighter than everyone else."

Eventually, she tells me, she recovered herself sufficiently to strike up a conversation with the new girl who'd rendered her speechless, and the two discovered they had more in common than Shannon at least might have anticipated.

"Both Mancs. Both from messed-up families, though obviously it wasn't 'til later I found out all the shit about her parents dying and her having to go and live with her bitch of an auntie and that boyfriend who couldn't keep his greasy fucking hands to himself. And in for the same sort of thing: I wasn't dealing like she was, but I was using, and I was off my tits the night I glassed that arsehole at the pub who got me put away. Not that I really regret *that*: this was before MeToo and men like him starting to be held a bit more accountable, but to this day, if a young girl told me she'd been followed to the bathroom by a bloke in his thirties who started grabbing her and wouldn't let go, I'd probably tell *her* to pick up the first sharp object she could reach and grind it in his face, as well."

There was also, crucially, one other experience Becky and Shannon shared.

"Gay, both of us. I didn't realise *she* was until she said it – my gaydar wasn't exactly a well-oiled machine back then – but I assume she knew about me before she sat down next to me. *Everyone* knew about me. I only started getting a clue about *her* when she dropped in stuff about her ex-girlfriend and *The L Word*. She told me afterwards she felt like she had to go in heavy-handed, or I never would've picked up on it."[3]

The girls hit it off, and – to Shannon's surprise, even in the hot-house atmosphere of the YOI, where relationships tended to accelerate at a rapid pace and burn out just as quickly – soon became an item.

"Becky took the lead. I wasn't this fragile little flower she took advantage of... I mean, I was in fucking *prison*, wasn't I? But for all my bullshit, I'd never actually had a girlfriend before, and I knew fuck-all about relationships. She had to do everything: kiss me, hold my hand, find somewhere for us to go so we could... you know. She even had to *tell* me we were going out, because I wasn't sure what the fuck was happening between us. Until she said it, I thought we were just messing around. That *she* was just messing around with *me*, for something to do."

They dated – "if you can call it that when you're inside," Shannon laughs – for the duration of Becky's sentence. And they were, at least as Shannon describes it, "completely in

---

3.  I really felt for her here. I have a feeling I was the same around girls I liked until I hit my twenties. Though obviously the cultural references then were more kd lang than Kate Moennig – G.

love. Or completely in what you *think* love is, when you're that age: everything dead intense, dead serious. And fucking hell, when we argued! We'd stand there *screaming* at each other over basically nothing. *You never listen to me* and *I saw you checking out that skinny bitch round the pool table*, every kind of stupid shit you can think of. Then we'd make up, and it'd be like fucking Romeo and Juliet again. *I love you so much* and *I'll never leave you*, making plans about where we'd live and what sort of dog we'd adopt once we got out. Stupid shit." She shakes her head; ruefully or fondly, I'm not sure which. "So fucking stupid."

When Shannon was released on licence, in 2010, she was placed in a hostel back in Manchester, some fifty miles from Willoughby. With no mobile phone, and unable to afford the train fare for visits, she assumed, despite the promises they'd made to one another while in custody, that Becky would soon forget her, and move on to another girl still incarcerated with her. Time, Shannon observes, "is different inside. Slower. A week can feel like a year, sometimes; like you're listening to a podcast and everything's running at half-speed, but you can't skip ahead, you have to wait it out."

She was taken aback therefore when, three months later, Becky – released from Willoughby early, on electronic tag – arrived at the same hostel, immediately sought out Shannon, and declared herself elated to have found her; to be reunited, finally, with the girl she called "my future wife."

"We just sort of... picked up where we left off," Shannon says. "Chris, who managed the hostel, she didn't like it – I think she thought we were bad for each other, or Becky was bad for *me*. That she'd drag me down, or whatever. But there was fuck all Chris or anyone could do about it, at the end of the day, except stop us going into one another's rooms... and I'm assuming you've met teenagers before, so you'll know that does exactly fucking nothing. We just found other places to be. Waited until she went off-shift to get into bed with each other."

Six months on, Becky's tag was removed; six months after *that*, Shannon completed her probation period, and the girls were free to leave the hostel – and the city.

"She had this thing about moving to London." Shannon's attention is drawn, for a second, to the skyline outside the window of her tenth-floor flat: the view of Docklands and the river, the cantilevered Modernisms of Canary Wharf. "I never was sure why. I got why she wanted out of Manchester, believe me, with the history both of us had there. I'd have been happy enough in York or Huddersfield – I didn't see why we had to run away to the other end of the country, especially when it was so fucking expensive. You couldn't argue with Becky when she was set on some-thing, though. Or... you could argue, but you couldn't *win*. You could shout the odds, but she'd always get her way in the end. And it wasn't like I had much of a case for us staying put, even if I'd wanted to make one. It was only agency work I was doing, warehouse stuff: processing and order picking, that sort of shit, and I was bored out of my brain, living for break-times so I could go and get fucked up in the bathroom or smoke a bit of weed out the fire escape. Becky wasn't even working, just signing on and pretending she was doing an Access course at college. She had a bit of money, but I never knew where it came from. I should've asked," she adds, quietly, "but I didn't want to know. I just... didn't want to know. You know?"

And so, the girls, still not out of their teens, decamped to the capital: Becky's "bit of money" and what little Shannon had saved from her factory jobs buying them the deposit and the first three months' rent, on a room in a shared house in Cricklewood.

"It was fucking grim," Shannon recalls. "Worse than the hostel in some ways. A galley kitchen, and one tiny bathroom covered in mould, shared between six of us: me and Becky, the Lithuanian couple in the room next door, a chemistry student from one of the unis who was renting out the box room, and this old bloke, Frankie, who slept downstairs in what should've been the living room. They get away with fucking murder, London landlords."

Her current apartment – so clean, spacious and well-appointed by contrast with her former residence – belongs, she tells me, to her ex-partner: a fashion designer who's based most of the year in Milan, and who charges Shannon only nominal rent while she's away. "No way would I be able to afford it otherwise," Shannon says. "Like I said: I've been fucking lucky."

Such luck was in shorter supply in the Cricklewood days, however. For the first year she and Becky lived in the city, neither girl worked: Shannon surviving on benefits supplemented with a few hundred pounds made here and there through trading on eBay, and Becky on a combination of Jobseeker's Allowance and those other "bits of money" of unspecified provenance.

"Did I think she was dealing again?" Shannon replies, when I ask. "Maybe. Maybe I *hoped* she was dealing, because it was a better option than some of the other things she could've been doing to get her hands on cash like that. We never had more gear in than we could use, so she definitely wasn't keeping any of it back for us, if she was. All our stuff, we bought off this posh Goth bloke she knew in Camden, Tobey. But if she *was* dealing... that would've explained a lot. She did a lot of sneaking around: always going out but not telling me *where* she was going, snatching her phone away if she thought I was trying to look at who was texting her... I used to accuse her of cheating on me all the time. *All* the time. We'd have some proper blazing rows about it. She'd always deny it, too – tell me she wasn't interested in anyone else, and I needed to just trust her, instead of getting paranoid."

In London as in Willoughby, their relationship was defined in large part by its volatility: arguments and breakup threats and dramatic reconciliations, conducted in a haze of drink and Class A substances, even when, eventually, Shannon was able to secure work in the kitchens of a fast-food restaurant in Holloway. It continued in this vein for several years – longer, frankly, than I might have expected a partnership like theirs to endure.

Only when they decided together to get clean, in the Christmas of 2015, did things begin to change between them.

"She got into a detox unit," Shannon says. "This in-patient place in Finchley; charity-run, not NHS, so a bit fucking nicer than your usual drying-out clinic. More meditation and morning yoga than a hospital bed and a bucket to be sick in when you're withdrawing. I don't know how she talked her way in – they normally only take you when you're really bad, liver transplant bad, and she was basically functional – but that was her all over. Magnetic, like I said."

Becky stayed in the unit, Shannon tells me, for 21 days – declaring herself drug- and alcohol-free upon discharge. Shannon, meanwhile, had been doing her own solo-detox in their rented room in Cricklewood, with neither medical supervision nor peer-group support to draw on; an undertaking which proved rather less successful than Becky's.

"Things weren't the same after that," she says. "I was a

mess, could barely get myself up and washed in the morning, but Becky was... different. It wasn't just that she'd stopped using. It was like her personality had... not changed, because she was still definitely herself, but *evolved*, maybe? And not in a good way. More like... all the worst bits of her started rising to the surface. Bits that had always been there, but that you didn't notice as much before, because the *other* bits – the sweet, kind, funny bits – were there as well, to balance them out."

*Which were what?* I ask. *How did these differences manifest?*

"She got..." Shannon hesitates - as if she's wary, even now, of badmouthing the girl who once meant so much to her. "She got mean. Started making these... comments to me, whenever I pissed her off: calling me names, shit like that. Telling me I was letting myself down, stopping myself from being the person I was supposed to be, because I was weak. Weak, and..."

She looks, for a moment, acutely embarrassed; so much so that I'm almost afraid to prompt her to continue.

"I sound fucking mental," she goes on eventually. "But some of what she said, it was sort of... homophobic. Some of the names she'd call me. I should think you can guess the sort of stuff I'm on about? You must've heard it all yourself at one time. Only *she* wasn't shouting it at me in the street or at some fucking Britain First rally or whatever. She was saying it to me in bed, after we'd been cuddling and... stuff. In the bathroom, after I'd got out the shower, or at the supermarket, if I put my arm 'round her when she was reaching for... I don't know, a tin of beans or something.

"Part of me would be like, what are you saying that for? Because she must've known it'd hurt me, her calling me a fucking dyke or telling me to *stop being so gay* when I wasn't doing anything different than I ever had with her. And another part of me would be like, hang on a minute: that's *you* as well. You're as queer as I am. You were literally.... sorry, I know this is a bit crude... you were literally going down on me five minutes ago. Now I'm *too gay* for you? What the fuck?"

It sounds to me, though I daresay Shannon has already puzzled as much out for herself, like classic projection; a bog-standard externalisation of self-hate, albeit of the kind more often observed in older closet-cases than in twentysomething girls who are already out and proud.

The *timing* of this particular sudden-onset bout of internalised homophobia, however, is interesting, inextricably linked as it appears to be with Becky's stay at the detox unit.

Does Shannon, I wonder, happen to remember which charity it was that ran the clinic?

"Put the pieces together as well, did you?" She smiles – not happily, but with what I take to be the satisfaction of someone who no longer blames herself for past actions beyond her control. "I do remember, yeah. It was a Christian one: In God's Hands. They're not around anymore, they were shut down by the Charity Commission a couple of years ago. Can you guess why?"

I shrug, but it's a rhetorical gesture: I have a strong sense already of what Shannon is about to say.

"Conversion therapy – the *pray the gay away* kind. Only they were badging it as rehab."

# GOD'S HANDS

In its prime, the registered charity In God's Hands operated seven drug and alcohol rehabilitation clinics across the UK – including East Finchley's Goldenrod Centre, into which Becky Cooper was admitted in January 2016.

We can't know for certain what happened to Becky specifically during her stay, although perhaps we could hazard a guess, given her subsequent treatment of her partner and apparently altered conception of her own sexuality and identity.

We can, however, refer to the personal testimonies of several former in-patients submitted to LGBTQ+ support service Gateways, and thereafter to police and the UK Charities Commission in 2019 – testimonies which led directly to the closure of all seven IGH-run treatment centres, the resignation of IGH CEO Martin Porter, and ultimately the dissolution of IGH itself via the invocation of the 2016 Charities (Protection and Social Investment) Act. These testimonies make for powerful, if distressing reading, and give some insight into the style and substance of the "therapeutic" practices implemented at the Goldenrod Centre and its sister sites.

Those undergoing treatment, Gateways reports, were subjected to what one former patient, ex-crystal meth addict Jacques, described as "brainwashing":

"Mandatory group prayer meetings, they made us do three times a day: before breakfast, after lunch, and just before bed. We were all exhausted anyway, because most of us were in some stage of withdrawal and genuinely physically sick, but they still managed to schedule the meetings for when we'd be most vulnerable: when we were hungry, drained already from the regular therapy sessions, or just ready to pass out and sleep for ten hours.

"There'd be readings from the Bible, obviously. Usually, it would be one of the counsellors picking passages from Romans or Corinthians. Then they'd get us to "go deeper" – that was what they called it. To say what we thought had driven us into addiction, what shame and guilt we were trying to run away from by self-medicating... and then find a way to tie it back to our 'deviated thinking.'"

"Not everyone in my intake was queer. Some were straight and married, and I think one guy might've been asexual. But the God's Hands people were obsessed with this idea that we were all sinners, that we'd all deviated from the path of righteousness and needed to be broken and remade until we were the right shape again. And for the queer people in my group – that was me, two other gay guys, this one lesbian and a bisexual girl who was super young, too young to be in a place like that – our queerness was definitely the sin, the deviation... and as far as God's Hands were concerned, that made it the reason we were drinking and drugging, too.

"You eradicate one sickness, you wipe away the sin, and

you cure the others with it. That was the way they looked at things. So, by making us less queer, making us pull our queerness out of ourselves by the root, they were making us into the sort of people who wouldn't *want* to drink or snort Tina anymore, who wouldn't *need* to drown out the urges we knew, deep down, were sinful."

Jacques also recalls the one-on-one "treatments" to which he was subjected.

"I got assigned this young guy, Daniel, to work with on what they called *reparative therapy*: their version of conversion therapy. I don't know what happened to all the others in my group, what sort of therapies *they* got, but mine was basically him asking me about my childhood and my relationship with my dad, trying to get me to admit that I was gay because my parents got divorced and I was reaching out for other men because I was looking for a father figure. It was the most textbook cod-psychology stuff you can imagine, stuff I know now has been completely discredited. Even then most of me sort of knew it was a load of crap, but I was in such a bad way trying to detox, paranoid as well as sick, that I'd have believed about anything that came with a guarantee of making me feel better.

"That was their whole model, at God's Hands. Getting you while you were at your weakest, so they could turn you into the sort of person they thought you should be."

It's a small mercy that IGH and "clinics" like it no longer operate in the UK – although successive Conservative governments, at the time of writing, have continued to drag their heels on the implementation of a full legal ban on conversion therapy, particularly as it affects trans and gender nonconforming individuals.

We shouldn't be surprised, however, that a young woman like Becky Cooper, already vulnerable on entering the program, emerged from her stay at IGH Finchley so radically changed. Nor perhaps should we be so terribly shocked, given the treatment she likely endured there, about some of the life-altering (and ultimately life-ending) decisions she made thereafter.

Shannon reaffirms Paula Deal's assertion that Becky first met her eventual husband, Brendan Cooper, via a mutual drug-world acquaintance, prior to her stint at IGH, and not at any of the Alcoholics or Narcotics Anonymous meetings all three attended from 2016 onwards.

Cooper, as Shannon remembers him from their early meetings, was "just some bloke. Not an obvious dickhead like some of them you'd get hanging 'round that scene, but nothing special, either. Very... standard. Average looking, averagely interesting, didn't say anything wildly offensive about lesbians, or women in general. I'm not even sure I'd have been able to tell you who he was, if he hadn't..." The smile she's been wearing until this point, perhaps for my benefit, fades. "Fucking awful dress sense, though," she adds, with only a modicum of bitterness. "Never saw him in anything but acid-wash jeans and football shirts. Should've known he was dodgy, just from that."

When Becky ended their relationship in the summer of 2016, Shannon says, there was no mention of Cooper – and not so much as an inkling on Shannon's part that he might have been involved in the breakup in any capacity.

"Not even a little bit. I thought there might've been *someone* else, the way she'd been with me – distant, cold, kind of mean. Pulling away. But I assumed it was another girl, because why wouldn't I? She was gay. She'd never been anything *other* than gay. If she ever fancied anyone, flirted with anyone, even when I'd thought in the past that maybe she'd gone out to meet someone else while I was at work or she'd been messing about with them behind my back... it was always girls, women. That she'd run off with a bloke... it wasn't even on the top 100 of things I'd ever worried about."

Becky's departure from their Cricklewood house-share was abrupt – and at first, Shannon says, came as a mild relief.

"She cleared all her stuff out while I was at work, the day after she told me she was leaving. And to be honest, the first thing I thought when I got home and saw everything gone was: okay, then. We hadn't been getting on, things had obviously been going to shit for a while... so maybe it was for the best that she'd been the one to pull the plug, when I hadn't had the guts to do it.

"I carried on like that for probably a fortnight: sort of sad and mopey, smoking a ton of weed on my own and listening to Joni fucking Mitchell until I bawled my eyes out, but basically alright. Then the letters started coming. Serious letters, from about four different banks I'd never heard of, all of them wanting repayments on loans I was supposed to have taken out, but hadn't."

Becky, as you may have guessed, was responsible for these loans: loans she'd taken out in Shannon's name, using Shannon's identification but without her knowledge, over the three months preceding their breakup. Together, they totalled almost twenty thousand pounds. The interest rates alone were cripplingly high.

"My head was spinning," Shannon says now. "I didn't know what the fuck was going on. When I'd got myself together enough, I rang one of the banks, though I couldn't tell you which one, and when I eventually got to speak to a person instead of a fucking automated message, they told me they couldn't tell me anything because I didn't know the passwords or the telephone banking login details. So, I was like, what the fuck? You can't tell me anything about this loan that's *in my fucking name, that you're asking me to pay for?* What sort of *Black Mirror* bullshit is this?

"They didn't even answer. Just hung up on me."

When, several similarly frustrating phone calls later, she was able to locate and travel to one of the few staffed physical branches of the largest of three banks, in Brondesbury, Shannon finally figured out what had happened, and how she'd been defrauded.

"One of the managers took me into his office and actually *showed* me on his computer when the loan was taken out, when it was signed off, and what ID they would've needed to approve it. I kept telling him: no, that's not right, I never did that. And he asks me: well, does anyone else have access to your birth certificate or your passport?

"And then it clicks. What must've gone on, that it must've been Becky who did it – applied for a bunch of fucking loans, pretending to be me, then taken the money and fucking ran.

"The bank manager must've seen the look on my face and noticed I'd had some sort of fucking revelation, because he was all, like: are you okay? Do you need me to contact our fraud team?

"And I couldn't think of what to say to him, what I was

supposed to fucking *do* about my girlfriend, my *ex*-girlfriend shafting me for twenty grand? So, I just said: no, you're alright. And then I was up and out the fucking door, trying not to have a panic attack in the middle of Kilburn fucking High Road."

Wary of police after her previous incarceration, and not wanting—despite her growing anger—to implicate Becky in any criminal proceedings that might land *her* back in detention, Shannon reacted, once that initial panic had faded, with unexpected cool-headedness: changing her bank details, contacting the debt management charity Control for help in devising a manageable repayment plan... and taking steps to get the money back from Becky directly.

"I started asking around people we knew – not her friends, I assumed *they* wouldn't tell me where she'd gone, but acquaintances. Blokes who might've seen her around since she left, and have a rough idea of where she was living. And that was how I found out what she'd done. That she'd not just taken the money – she'd used it to shack up with that cunt [Cooper] in the fucking countryside."

After a fortnight or more of (by her own admission) "bombarding" Becky with texts and phone calls that went unacknowledged, Shannon was able to persuade one of these acquaintances to part with Becky's – and Cooper's – new address: a house in the picturesque Hertfordshire village of Colney Heath, a short drive from St Albans and a hundred social-economic light years from Cricklewood. She set out to confront the new couple almost immediately.

"I get there, and it's this lovely little semi down a cul-de-sac. Not a palace, alright, but a fuck of a lot better than the dump *we'd* been living in. Must've cost, I don't know, a couple of grand a month to rent? A couple of grand of *my fucking money*. I could feel my piss boiling even while I was stood outside on the pavement, trying to get up the nerve to ring the doorbell."

It was Brendan, not Becky, who answered the door. And Brendan who told Shannon, in no uncertain terms, to go away and leave them alone: that Becky had made her choice, that she'd chosen *him* and wanted to build a new life with *him*, and that she didn't need Shannon's "sickness" dragging her down when she was trying to move on and stay clean.

"His words: *sickness*. And I knew exactly what he fucking meant when he said it, because he fucking *spat* it at me. He might as well have called me a *dirty fucking dyke* and had done with it. But, you know... I didn't exactly have the headspace to think about that, there and then. So, I just said, *she owes me money*. And you know what he does then? He *sticks his hand in the pocket of those acid-wash fucking jeans* like he's reaching for his wallet, and he says, *how much?* Like I'm going to tell him it's a couple of fivers or something, and I'd pegged it down to the fucking sticks so I could get him to cough up a tenner.

"So, I laugh, because he's a fucking joke and the whole thing is fucking ridiculous, and I say, *it's a bit more than that, mate. Not sure even your M&S credit card's gonna cut it.* And he asks me *how* much, so I tell him. And then I tell him: *bad news about the new missus. 'Cause she took all of that out in my name – and if she did it to me, then she'll do the same to you when it suits her.*

"Can't say he took it well. I don't know if he believed me or not – I mean, as far as he was concerned, I was just some junkie lesbian he'd met a few times. It didn't matter to him I'd been with Becky, like, eight years by then, did it? So, he listens a bit to what I'm saying, about the loans and that...

then he snarls his face up, like he really *does* want to spit at me, calls me a fucking liar and slams the door in my face.

"Oh, and right before he does, he tells me: if I come back again when he's home, he'll ring the police. That they'll arrest me, and I'll get sent down again, like before.

"Lovely bloke he was, Brendan Cooper. Real fucking gent."

Startled by this threat, Shannon fled – only to return to Colney Heath a few days later, this time under the influence of alcohol and the synthetic cannabinoid spice.

"That isn't an excuse," she repeats. "I was off my fucking face, I'd been up all night, and I'd got myself so worked up it started to seem like a good idea. I'd been texting Becky pretty much every day since Cooper threatened to have me arrested, and she'd stopped even opening the texts, so I was a bit like: what else am I supposed to do here? Sit about smiling while she's shagging her new boyfriend and burning through the money I'm going fucking bankrupt trying to pay off? No. Just fucking *no*.

"I'd started to sober up a bit once I actually got to the house, enough that I didn't go steaming straight up to the door. I could see he was in, Cooper – there was a fucking Prius in the driveway, and Becky didn't even have a licence. And I knew he'd be on me if I rang the bell again, so I sort of... waited across the road. Went and stood behind this big tree and just *watched* the house. Stood there staring at it, like a proper stalker.

"Maybe half an hour I was there – could've been longer, who the fuck knows? – when the front door opens, and out steps Becky holding hands with that cunt [Cooper], both of them dressed up: her in heels and this blue maxi dress I'd never seen her in before that made her look like an extra from the fucking *Handmaid's Tale*, and him in this horrible blue suit that even *then* I could've told you came from Topman. They started out towards the Prius, so I got it in my head they'd drive off and I'd be able to sneak off without them seeing me... only they didn't get in. They kept walking, out the driveway and down to the end of the road. And I..." Shannon blushes, her shame and self-recrimination apparent even today. "I followed them. Kept far enough behind them that they didn't see me, and followed them all the way to where they were going."

Which was, to Shannon's great surprise, a church: the South Herts Chapel of Christ.

"I googled it, once I'd seen them go in. It's an evangelical place, part of this umbrella group called Allied Charismatics. You know about it, I assume, if you've been digging around already? They're evangelicals, *hardcore* evangelicals: anti-queer, anti-woke, anti-feminist... you name it. Even on the actual church's website, there's a load of stuff about *deviance* and *wickedness* and the traditional family being God's plan, whatever the fuck that means. I had an auntie growing up who was well in with the Jehovah's Witnesses and used to post copies of *Awake!* and *The Watchtower* through our letterbox... this church, I'm telling you, it was reading from the same fucking hymn book, excuse the pun.

"And I've just watched Becky, *my* Becky, who's never picked up a Bible in her life, walk right in there on the arm of some cheap-suited dickhead."

Shannon swipes at her eyes; almost, but not quite crying as she remembers.

"I was still mad at her for what she'd done, how she'd fucked me over – fucking raging at her, really. How could I not be? But also, I was thinking: *what have you done, Becks? What the fuck have you got yourself into?*"

Shannon made no direct contact with Becky or Cooper

that morning; nor was she able to reclaim even part of the money owed her. But she found herself falling, in the weeks and months that followed, into a self-destructive pattern: abstaining from drugs and alcohol while at work and in the evenings but succumbing to both at weekends, then phoning and texting Becky when intoxicated, alternately demanding the repayment of the money and begging her to come back. She would also, where her own finances allowed, take the Thameslink to Colney Heath: sometimes simply observing Cooper and Becky's new home from a distance, as she had on that first visit, and sometimes confronting them directly on their doorstep.

"He actually *did* call the police on me, in the end," she says. "Another Sunday, after they'd got back from that fucking church and caught me hanging around under the tree across the road. I scarpered before anyone came, if they even fucking bother coming out for shit like that, but sure enough, they came banging on *my* door a couple of days later, saying they'd had a report of me *making a nuisance of myself* in St Albans and asking what I was doing there. I told them: nothing, I was visiting a mate in Colney Heath and it was all a coincidence, bumping into Becky and that cunt when I did. Not that they believed a fucking word of it, but what were they going to do, arrest me for sitting under a tree on a public fucking footpath? So, they just did the usual, which was about all they *could* do: warned me to stay away from Becky, from both of them. Said it'd only get more serious if they had to come round and tell me that again, so I'd best keep clear of that bit of the Home Counties unless I wanted to go back inside. Then they left."

This official warning, and the threat of returning to prison, frightened Shannon sufficiently that she did as the police advised and stayed away from Colney Heath thereafter. The texts and phone calls continued for a while; but after a time, she tells me, even they lost their appeal.

"That twenty grand wasn't coming back, whatever I did. Anyway, I'm not even sure it was *about* the twenty grand by then. I was carrying around all this anger, all this bitterness... and I really *was* worried for her, jumping into something with a bloke – something so committed – and signing up to go and wash herself in the blood of fucking Christ. It wasn't exactly a coincidence all that happened right after she'd gone to rehab, was it? I didn't know about the In God's Hands shit then – nobody did, 'til it got shut down and everything came out in the news. But I could've told you *something* had gone on when she was in there. That they'd fucking *done* something to her head while she was trying to get herself clean."

With no chance of reclaiming the stolen loan money without officially implicating Becky, and with her funds and emotional reserves both severely depleted, Shannon focused instead on her own mental health and sobriety: entering therapy, cutting ties with drug-world friends and dealers, and throwing herself into the college course that would lead on to her apprenticeship. For a period, life was stable, if not always easy.

Until, that is, the Heart of Solomon murders brought the police once again to her door.

"I didn't even know they'd got married," she says, sombrely. "Let alone that they'd moved out of Colney to some fucking tradwife commune. Then to hear they've been murdered, that *she'd* been murdered, and to have the fucking dibble drag me down the cop shop for questioning, acting like they're my best mates one minute and asking me the next to tell the nice detective how I did it, how I fucking killed them... It was a lot to take in, you know what I mean? A fuck of a lot."

It seems unnecessary to retread the already familiar ground of what happened to Shannon in the days thereafter: the multiple police interrogations and the media witch-hunts, all compounding what I imagine to be her immense grief at learning that the woman she'd been with, *lived* with for close to a decade, had died in such appalling circumstances.

I would, however, like to understand a little more about Shannon's reaction to the Heart of Solomon community itself – and specifically, to Becky and Cooper having ended up there in the last months of their lives.

We know now that it was through the Chapel of Christ, and by extension the Allied Charismatics, that Brendan Cooper met and became friendly with Freddie and Nadine Taylor – themselves members of an affiliated congregation. But what, in Shannon's opinion, would draw someone like Becky – apparently so headstrong, at least before her stay at IHG Finchley – to a Trad lifestyle in the first place? Or indeed to the sort of traditionalist ideology espoused by the Taylors?

"Fucked if I know." Shannon shakes her head, genuinely perplexed. "You might as well ask me what a lesbian, and she *was* a lesbian, no fucking doubt about it... what she was doing marrying a bloke, *any* bloke. None of it fits with the person I thought she was when we were together. Her going off with that cunt [Cooper], the two of them joining some fucking right-wing extremist cult so they could cosplay Terry and fucking June in a disused field... even her taking the money and skipping out on it, on *me* – it makes about as much fucking sense to me as if she'd been... I don't know, a fucking T-800 cyborg or something. As if she'd ripped off all her skin one day and shown me she had nothing but wires and metal underneath, instead of bones."

She winces – suddenly reminded, I suspect, of the circumstances of Becky's death, and the condition of her mutilated body *in* death.

"I have to think she just got a bit... lost," she adds, more quietly. "That's what I tell myself, when I start chewing it over and it's keeping me up at night: that Becks went into that place, that fucking detox centre, and they messed her up so badly with their fucking *therapy* she came out not knowing who she was or what she wanted. And that cunt Cooper, he was just... there. Something to grab onto; something that seemed solid in the way she thought she was looking for.

"It's the only way I can square it: that she was lost, and he just fucking... manipulated her into all of that, what went on after. The church, and the tradwife bollocks, and... you know. The rest of it."

Shannon elaborates no further on what *the rest of it* might mean, in this context, but I can hazard a guess to what she's referring. That is: those activities and predilections of Brendan Cooper's that came to light in the aftermath of his death, when a police forensics report summarising the contents of Cooper's personal laptop appeared in the inbox of TikTok influencer and self-described "investigative journalist" Cameron Huhne, sender unknown, its contents both graphically detailed and incriminating in the extreme.

And which, while certainly portraying Cooper as coercive and manipulative, throw into question – though I refrain from saying as much directly to Shannon – any straightforward framing of Becky as a wholly blameless victim of circumstance.

BRENDAN

I loathe Brendan Cooper.

It's accepted wisdom in British culture, I realise, that one ought to refrain from speaking ill of the dead. Likewise, it's standard practice, in investigative journalism as in ethnographic research, to approach one's subjects openly, dispassionately and without judgement: to understand, and where possible to empathise, no matter how repugnant one finds the individuals involved.

I've tried, inasmuch as I've been able, to abide by these tenets thus far in the writing of this book: when profiling the abusive wife-beater Jason Wilson and the opportunistic racist Freddie Taylor, for example, or when interviewing the ultraconservative antifeminist "Auntie" Annamaria Ainsworth.

But Brendan Cooper disgusts me, and I'd prefer, in the interests of transparency, to admit as much upfront.[1]

---

1. Helen – please tell me if I've gone too far here. I worry a little that digging into Brendan Cooper in particular has dredged up some long-buried stuff about my mother and Johnny Mahoney and the Free People's

If you've followed the Heart of Solomon murders and their aftermath in the press, you'll have a sense already of why this might be. If not, then the paragraphs and chapters that follow will, I imagine, provide all the answers you need.

The facts of Cooper's early life are prosaic enough. Born in March 1990, and 29 years old in September 2019, when Dev Thakar discovered his castrated body amid the bloodbath that had been the Taylors' dining room, Cooper grew up in the East Midlands market town of Chesterfield, the second son of local GP Andrew Cooper and his wife Rhianna, a veterinary nurse and former Düsseldorf Opera Company soprano.

Available biographies, notably Paula Deal's, point to the young Cooper's achievements in creative art and performance, including prizes won in painting and poetry recital at the Nuneaton Festival of Arts and the Derbyshire Open.[2] By his teens, however, he'd already begun to drink heavily, including during classes at St. David's, the private all-boys' school in Bakewell he attended – and from which, according to Deal's account, he was sent home more than once for alcohol-fuelled misconduct. Poor GCSE results were superseded by poorer-still A Levels in biology, chemistry and environmental science and, though he was able to enter a Medical Physiology BSc program at King's College London via Clearing, his academic attainments and eventual degree were lacklustre, no doubt in part as a consequence of his excessive drinking and burgeoning cocaine use. Twice he was hospitalised with alcohol poisoning, both times in the second year of his studies; he also received

---

Collective, for obvious reasons. I'm not sure how easily I can stay objective – G.

2.   Deal, P. *The Keepers of Wives*

police cautions for drunk and disorderly behaviour, and in his final year was interviewed, though never charged, in relation to a sexual assault on a fellow student.[3]

Publicly available information on Cooper's movements immediately after his graduation from King's is mostly scant. We know he lived for a period in a shared house in Vauxhall, and then another in Streatham; we know he worked, and was frequently fired from, a succession of low-paid jobs in retail, hospitality and manufacturing, often on zero-hour contracts.

We also know, from accounts given by those former friends and acquaintances willing to sell their stories to the tabloids, that he continued to drink, take cocaine and experiment with cheaper drugs – among them crack, benzodiazepines, mephedrone and the MDMA-like PMA – on a greater-than-regular basis.[4] Many of these he purchased from his friend Caspar Sandhu, the dealer through whom he was first introduced to Becky.

Quite why Becky should have been drawn to him after her stint at IHG remains, at least to me, something of a mystery. Though moderately attractive by the prevailing standards of white, heteronormative masculinity, at least in those photographs of him to which I've been privy, Cooper was no matinee idol; his body that bit too lean and his triangular, thin-lipped face disdainful rather than approachable. Nor was he, if Shannon Delaney's characterisation of him as "just some bloke" is to be believed, especially charismatic; indeed, those acquaintances of Cooper to whom Paula Deal spoke recall him as "moody" and apt to "fade into the back-

<hr>

3. Ibid.
4. Wolfe, T. '"A Properly Hardcore Junkie": The Double Life of Tradwife Victim Cooper.' *The New Herald*, December 16, p1.

despite his propensity for erratic and antisocial behaviour when drunk or high, or both.[5]

A greater mystery still surrounds his conversion to evangelical Christianity, a decision which surprised even his immediate family – not least his older brother Phil, whom we'll meet in the next chapter.

Phil has his own explanations and hypotheses regarding Cooper's motive for getting clean – and for Cooper himself entering a detox facility in early 2016, albeit one less ideologically loaded one than IGH.

Cooper's later-in-life religiosity, however – his sudden-onset enthusiasm for Trad values and his move, along with Becky, to the Heart of Solomon... all of these, Phil finds both puzzling and sickening.

Though perhaps not quite so puzzling, nor quite so sickening, as those *other* revelations about his brother's conduct and character that came to public attention only weeks after his death.

------

5.  Deal, P. *The Keepers of Wives*, pp92-93.

PHIL COOPER

"I can say, categorically, that we've never been a religious family," Phil Cooper tells me. "Dad's dad was Irish, and he was raised sort of... culturally Catholic, I suppose you'd call it, but he doesn't practise. And mum's the staunchest atheist you'll ever meet. She makes Richard Dawkins look like Pope Benedict, if you dare get her started on intelligent design."

This disavowal of organised religion isn't wholly unexpected, coming from a man who presents as Phil does. A bulky, generously bearded white guy with a hemp shirt unbuttoned to the chest and more string bracelets than I can count circling his thick wrists, he wouldn't be out of place around a campfire at Glastonbury or gluing himself to the Millennium Bridge in protest at the climate crisis. His accent betrays his upper-middle-class background: private school, bilingualism earned through summer holidays in Provence, undergraduate and master's degrees at St. Andrew's. But I'm left in no doubt, after a few minutes in his company, that he wouldn't hesitate to apologise for the good fortune life has afforded him, were I to bring it up. He is, I sense, well-versed in checking his privilege.

He lives in Bristol, where he works in the product development department of a green energy company, and it's in Bristol that we meet – in the basement of a vegan cafe owned by his friends Kirk and Nathan, who greet me warmly on my arrival and proceed to ply us both with coffee and plant-based scones for the duration of our stay.

I ask Phil, once the formalities are out of the way and our interview proper has commenced, if he and Brendan were close – and if the conservative, and ultimately evangelical trajectory of his brother's later life was out of character, or accorded with Phil's recollections of the Brendan he grew up with. Was Brendan always religious, I wonder – or was his conversion a sharp and unforeseen right-turn?

"He wasn't remotely interested in church as a kid," Phil insists – his family's wider atheistic credentials having been established to his satisfaction. "And if that *had* been a thing he was into, something he'd wanted to pursue, I can't see mum or dad agreeing to take him to any sort of... service. They're science people. They like evidence, not homilies and transubstantiation. We went to Sacré-Cœur once when I was ten, so mum could look at the architecture, but it wasn't what you'd call a spiritual experience."

Some former addicts, I observe, report throwing themselves headlong into extreme religiosity after kicking drugs or alcohol – effectively replacing one addiction with another.[1] Might this have been the case for Brendan?

---

1. I saw this myself, with my mother: on those rare occasions when she'd stop drinking – usually for no longer than a couple of weeks – she'd get *very* into some arcane hobby or other, and fill the flat with the necessary (and unnecessary) accoutrement of whatever hobby it was. Then she'd relapse, and I'd spend the next few months having to navigate stacks of half-finished macramé or essential oils or whatever whenever I opened the front door – G.

Phil takes a full minute to consider this; so long that I begin to wonder whether this is his rather passive way of ducking the question.

"Maybe," he says finally. "But the truth is, I don't really *know*. Brendan and I, and Josh - that's our younger brother, he's in Burundi now with Médecins Sans Frontières - we were together a lot as kids, the way you are when you're all stuck next to each other in the same house, but we didn't always have a great deal in common, if you see what I mean. We're quite different people. I'm pretty laid-back, and I tend not to get too worked up about things, where Josh is quite introverted and cerebral, usually. He mostly holed himself up in his room until he moved out for uni. And Brendan... well. Is there a word for "miserable dickhead half the time and appalling show-off the rest, but you can't tell him to go fuck himself because he's family and your mum wouldn't take too kindly to it"? I'm sure there must be, in German."

Phil smiles, though I'm inclined under the circumstances to read it as something more akin to a grimace.

"We never did get on particularly well. It wasn't that he ever did anything particularly awful or outré. Then, at least. But he could be very unkind, when he thought other people weren't looking. Not to me – I was always bigger than him, and I was very into kickboxing and hockey back then, so I assume he thought I'd have broken his nose if he'd tried anything. But absolutely to Josh, sometimes. Making fun of him, throwing away his exercise books to make it seem like he hadn't done his homework, hiding his PE kit on the days he needed it... that sort of thing. Josh is quite an anxious soul, needs everything organised just so, and he can get very stressed when his routines are disrupted. Brendan liked to play on that. To send him spiralling, just for the fun of it.

"There were other things, too. Again, not things I saw

myself," he adds, as if to pre-empt any request I might make for specific dates and times. "Rumours, really. But the school we all went to, St. David's, it was quite a small place, 500 boys or so all in, so if someone did something, or had a reputation for doing something... it got around the corridors quite quickly."

*And Brendan had a reputation? For doing what?*

Phil – big, laid-back, kautuka-wearing Phil – seems suddenly, desperately embarrassed.

"Do you know rugby?" he says, practically squirming in his seat.

No, I tell him – unfortunately not. My wife occasionally makes me sit through a football match when it's an important one, but I tend to fall asleep on the sofa during the national anthem. Why does he ask?

"But you know what a scrum is?"

Just about, I say, recalling the groups of mud-stained men I encounter from time to time when I'm out for a Saturday run around our local sports field. The tall, heavyset guys built much like Phil, huddling together and collapsing on top of one another in pursuit of a ball I can never quite make out through the compressed flesh-wall of their bodies.

"St. David's, where we went, it was big on rugby. Everyone played, even if they were shit at it. And Brendan... he'd try to *do* things to the other kids, when they got into a scrum. Hurt them, but... *sexually* hurt them, you know? Twist their nipples. Dig his nails into their balls. Stick his fingers up their arses when they were underneath him and couldn't get away. I never once saw him at it, as I say. But he had reputation for doing it. Some of the nastier kids, the bullies, they found it bloody *hysterical*; I daresay to them he was some kind of folk hero. Everyone tried to avoid getting near him in a game, though, especially in a scrummage. They all knew what might happen if they didn't.

"Brendan wasn't gay. I'd swear to that on anything you like: the Bible, the Quran, the Bhagavad Gita... whatever you've got. I'm bi myself, and I never got even the tiniest hint of a queer vibe off him. I don't think it was that he enjoyed *touching* the other guys, per se. I think he just liked humiliating them. Causing them pain – but perhaps a little bit of shame, as well? Because, well... it's different, isn't it? Saying *another boy squeezed my ball sack until it ruptured* isn't quite the same as saying *he dirty-tackled me too hard and it broke my collarbone*, even though it sort of *should* be, because both of them are things some other bastard *did* to you, aren't they? But no-one at that age wanted anyone else to think they might be even a little bit gay, back then... maybe they still don't, I don't know. The homophobia was rampant at schools like St. David's, absolutely rampant. And if you'd told someone, even a teacher, that another boy had grabbed you, that he'd *done* things to you... the *best* you'd have got back would have been that teacher telling you to *shut up about it and move on*. More than likely you'd have had other kids saying you'd enjoyed it, that you *must have* enjoyed it if you let it happen and you didn't fight back.

"Which is why it was all just rumours, I suppose, and never anything more formal. People, women, they talk a lot now about whisper networks; keeping each other safe through sharing gossip about which men to avoid and whatnot. Well... we had our own whisper network at St. David's. I'm not sure how effective it was... but you'd like to think it kept at least a few of the younger ones away from boys like Brendan. You'd like to hope."

You can see why Freddie Taylor and the Heart of

Solomon might have appealed to him, I say, unable to stop myself – my efforts at journalistic objectivity, or even feigned sympathy for the dead man, falling for a moment by the wayside.

"Exactly!" Phil agrees, seizing on the point before I can formulate an apology. "That's what it's all about, isn't it, that kind of ultra-traditionalism? Domination. It's men enjoying power over other people, over women. Yes, I should imagine Brendan would have found that very much to his tastes."

This seems an opportune moment to bring up that for which Brendan Cooper is perhaps best known, beyond the bizarre circumstances of his murder and the undeniably gruesome condition of his body in death: his grotesque treatment and sexual abuse of women, documented in such unremitting detail in the police report leaked to Cameron Huhne, and subsequently reiterated in interview with journalist Samantha McMenaman by beauty influencer and former sex worker Mihaela Popescu, of whom more later.

First, though, I want to understand a little more about how Phil feels about what came before: about Brendan's addictions, his marriage to Becky and subsequent religious conversion, and the couple's move to the Heart of Solomon community. How aware was Phil of the extent of his brother's substance abuse issues, before Brendan entered detox? How involved was he, or any of their family, in Brendan's recovery?

"Involved?" Phil hunches over his now-empty coffee mug, awkward again. "I didn't even know he had a problem. He got himself in trouble with the drinking at school... I know it kept the olds awake at night whenever he got himself suspended, and dad was in pieces when Bren went off at him and mum for asking if he was okay after he'd fucked up his GCSEs. The whole thing was awful, actually:

I was up in the loft, hanging out the window having a smoke, and I could hear him screaming at them with two floors between us. I suppose I didn't really see him getting off his face as... something he struggled with, as such? I rather thought he enjoyed it. The being drunk, but also, I don't know... the freedom it gave him to be unpleasant to people?

"I may be wrong, of course. It may be that I'm doing him a great disservice, and that he very much *was* struggling, and the bottle was one of his coping mechanisms – his way of masking, as they say. You must take everything I tell you as... only how it seemed to me, at the time. From a distance of twenty years, remember.

"And to that end: there is *something* I've considered since. Considered often, to be perfectly frank. I was talking to my wife about it only this morning, before I set off to meet you, and that wasn't the first time she's listened to me chew it over."

*Chew* what *over?*

"We know Brendan had some... let's say darker impulses. That he liked to hurt people. What if *that* was what he was masking when he drank? What if getting out of his head was his way of burying some of the... more unpleasant things he might have wanted to do to people, or might have done already?

"I wasn't around for his rock-bottom moment, with the coke and things. Or when he took himself off to rehab. I was working in Berlin, and my then-partner was based in Amsterdam so I wasn't flying home terribly often, and mum and dad, I've since discovered... they kept a lot of things from us, me and Josh. Trying to shield us, I suppose; filtering out the bad news so *we* wouldn't worry. They're very much of *that* generation.

"But let's say Bren *was* masking with drugs and alcohol, that he *was* using them to suppress... instincts he wasn't proud of. Wouldn't religious fundamentalism, the Tradwife kind of religious fundamentalism, be the perfect place to run to, once he'd given them up? That brand of Christianity, the toxic strain that people like Freddie Taylor want to straitjacket the rest of us into... it normalises misogyny. It tells men they *should* be aggressive, that they *should* want to subjugate and tyrannise, even if only in their own homes, and that wanting to is a normal, natural aspect of masculinity, and it's the rest of us who've gone astray. Really, if you ran a church that believed in all of that – or you were high up in one, like the Taylors – and you were actively recruiting men to help set up your Brave New Patriarchy: wouldn't you think you'd struck gold if you came across a guy like Brendan? A junkie and a drunk with a hole in his life where the drugs and whiskey used to be, who already had a taste for hurting people, and who'd lap it up if you told him he was allowed to be sadistic, *encouraged* to be sadistic, just as long as he toed your church's line and only did what he needed to do when the curtains were drawn?"

Is it Becky he's referring to there, I ask – or someone else? Does he believe Brendan was abusing his wife, as well as other women?

"Maybe. I met Becky... perhaps six or seven times, altogether? Including at their wedding, which I must say was a profoundly uncomfortable experience. The vows were... I suppose what you'd expect of a fundamentalist congregation. A lot of talk of duty and submission and God cleaving everyone together. Thankfully Sofia [Phil's wife] and I were at a table with mum and dad and Josh and his girlfriend Zanele, so there wasn't much need to mix with the church people once the handshakes and the *thank you for comings* were out of the way. Good thing, too: mum actually laughed when she saw the Bible verses they'd stashed in the champagne glasses. *Very* awkward stuff.

"What I'm trying to say is: none of us knew Becky, really. She came out of nowhere, to a large extent. One day Brendan was single, as far as I was concerned, and the next he was engaged to this girl none of us had heard about before.

"She seemed rather bland to me, if we're being brutally honest. Not terribly awash with personality, though of course you must factor in that we were virtual strangers, and is anyone *really* themselves hanging out with the in-laws? What the dynamic was between her and Brendan at home... perhaps it's anyone's guess. Much of what I think now is what I've inferred from what's come out since, about Brendan and..."

He quietens, and I wish dearly for a moment, given how obviously distressed this particular segment of our conversation makes him, that he'd thought to order something stronger than an oat milk latte.

"Those videos," he says, spinning his empty mug between his hands. "Becky was in them, wasn't she? And I know what the report said: that she was... an active participant in what Brendan did. That she held those women down, and so on. But what if it wasn't something she chose? What if Brendan coerced her, and what those videos showed was just the evidence of that coercion?"

It's impossible to know, I tell him – aware even as I say it that this is unlikely to make him feel any better at all.

# THE GIRLS IN THE VIDEOS

It didn't take long, once the police write-up of the videos found on Brendan Cooper's laptop had been sent to Cameron Huhne, for the videos themselves to enter the public domain. Though all constabularies involved in the investigation into the Heart of Solomon murders have vehemently denied culpability, with one anonymous source attributing both leaks to unnamed "civilian contractors," and though traces of all four videos have been purged on multiple occasions from the better-known porn and adult entertainment websites, all four can nevertheless be found and downloaded with relative ease to this day on many of the darkweb's less salubrious file-sharing platforms.

Like so many others, I have watched these videos; I have read the leaked report. And I have been left profoundly troubled by both experiences.

If I'm to stand by the original remit of this book and give as full an account as I'm able of the lives and backgrounds of all six Heart of Solomon victims, then it's necessary – I feel – to briefly outline the nature of the videos, for the benefit of those fortunate enough to have avoided encountering them directly. Those especially sensitive to scenes of sexual violence, however, are advised to skip over the paragraphs that follow.

All four videos are shot in what we now know to be the Heart of Solomon bedroom of Brendan and Becky Cooper: a neatly nondescript rectangle of nothing-space painted duck egg blue and cream, its centrepiece a king size bed furnished with pure-white linen. A large canvas wedding photo of Brendan and Becky hangs from one wall; from another, a framed Bible verse in cross-stitch, just about recognisable as Genesis 2:18.

*The LORD God said, "It is not good for the man to be alone. I will make a helper fit for him."*

Each video opens on essentially the same tableau: a young white woman, blonde and slim, splayed naked across the bed, her eyes closed and her body unmoving. She's still; so still, we might imagine her on first glance to be a corpse, though the steady undulation of her breastbone suggests on closer inspection that she is, after all, only unconscious. Her neck is angled away from the camera, such that her features are largely obscured.

She might be anyone.

Into the frame, in each video, come a man and a woman, whose features by contrast are extremely clear, and whom we recognise immediately as Brendan and Becky Cooper. Brendan is bare-chested, in briefs or tight-fitting boxer shorts. Becky wears lingerie: the same black camisole in every video.

Together, hand-in-hand, they approach the bed, and the unconscious woman on it.

At the bed, they separate. Becky, on her knees, positions herself at the headboard, and seizes the unconscious woman by the wrists – very much, as Phil Cooper observed, as if to hold her in place.

Brendan, his gaze apparently fixed on Becky, pulls down his underwear, spreads the unconscious woman's legs, insinuates himself between them, and rapes her.

One video lasts only ten minutes; another almost an hour. At no point in any video does the woman in question regain consciousness.

As those familiar with the Heart of Solomon story will know, it took the amateur sleuths of Reddit and Twitter scarcely a fortnight from the leak of the videos to identify three of the four women in shot, although the fourth remains unidentified at the time of writing.

Two of these have issued neither formal confirmation nor explicit denial of their presence in the videos, and there is nothing to be gained by my dragging their names back into the public sphere here. No doubt they'd prefer that I refrain from doing so.

The third woman, however, has been courageous enough to go public with her story: speaking with The Objective's Samantha McMenaman in what remains her only official interview on the matter.

Like the two other named women, Mihaela Popescu was previously a sex worker – and, like the others, she was contacted by the Coopers in the first instance via the escort website Ladies First.

The Coopers, Popescu says, booked her for an "out-call": paying £800 for an 8 hour "couples date" (Ladies First's rather euphemistic term for a paid threesome), originally scheduled to take place on a midweek evening at a budget hotel in central Nottingham.

At the last minute, however, the Coopers emailed to petition for a change of venue, apologising for the inconvenience, and requesting that Popescu visit them instead at their home at the Heart of Solomon site. Popescu, by her own admission "an admin fiend" who stored and meticulously filed all correspondence with her clients, was able to share the email exchange with McMenaman, who reproduced it in turn for The Objective. The tone throughout is formal, courteous, respectful; the Coopers – who show no interest in concealing their identities, signing themselves "Brendan and Rebecca" and sending the message from the email address "b.cooper@ crackle.com" – reiterate how much they're looking forward to meeting Popescu, and how grateful they are for her flexibility.

There was, as she tells McMenaman, nothing in the exchange to suggest she ought to be concerned; none of the warning signs she, as a woman whose personal safety depended in large part on her ability to sniff out potential predators ahead of a meeting, was well-versed in spotting. Only later, she says, did the red flags present themselves. And by then, there was little she could have done to heed them.

From here, I think, it's best to let Mihaela Popescu describe in her own words what happened on the night she visited the Coopers at the Heart of Solomon.[1]

"I told them I'd be coming in a taxi. And he [Brendan Cooper] says, fine, no problem – but the taxi can't drop you at the house. Our community is a tight-knit sort of place, nosy neighbours and that, so you can't be seen driving in or knocking at the door. People will ask questions.

---

1. Helen – I know Sam Mc reasonably well, and she's given me verbal permission for excerpts from the interview to be used in the body of the text here. Assume we'll have to get her to sign something more formal too before anything goes to print? – G.

"Okay, I tell him. You're not exactly the first client who's wanted to keep things discreet. How do you want to do this?

"And he says, we'll pick you up. Get the cab to drop you at this pub [the Golden Fleece in Kilmarsh, half a mile from the Heart of Solomon site] and we'll come and get you. Then you can drive home with us and no-one'll be any the wiser.

"We'll both wear white so you recognise us, he tells me, like we're in a war film and he'll be passing me a secret dossier under the table. Or you could just come and find me where I'm sitting, I say. You've seen my photos, you already know what I look like.

"And actually, it's a really nice pub, really quiet, with like three old men sinking pints at the bar and no other customers, so I see immediately when I get there that there's no danger of me getting lost in the crowd. [The Coopers] are *not* what I'd expected when they turn up, though.

"He'd told me they were young, both in their twenties, so quite a bit younger than my usual client base – and people usually want to make a good impression when they hire me, so I assumed they'd be decently well put-together, that they'd have made an effort with how they dressed. And actually, they *weren't* bad-looking, at all. She was more my type than he was, quite striking really, where he was more... meh. But what they were wearing... God. They looked like Jehovah's Witnesses or Mormons or something. Them people who stop you in the street to try to talk to you about Jesus.

"He's in these horrible jeans and a white blazer, like someone's dad at a golf club dinner. And she's got a white blouse on, this ruffled monstrosity buttoned up to the neck. Very Victorian schoolmistress. And I'm like, is it a fetish thing? Have they started the role play already? Are they gonna want *me* to dress up too?

"Anyway, they start talking, and they seem nice enough. A bit uptight, but that's very common with first timers, though it's usually the wife who's more nervous when it's couples. Not with them, though – he was squirmy, like his palms were sweating, but she was pretty chill. Like maybe it wasn't *her* first time, you get me?

"We have a drink in the pub, some very light chat. He tells me she's a housewife, and he does something in IT, managing a website for some guy he says is famous but who I've never heard of. Boring stuff, I'm thinking, if it's even true – and it's probably not, clients make all sort of shit up to try and impress you – but he's bragging about it like he's the Prime Minister's secretary or something.[2] Then the wife says, shall we head back to ours?

And off we go, in the car.

"He [Cooper] drives us to this little new estate that looks like it's been built in the middle of a cow field, and when we go to drive through it he tells me to duck down so no-one sees me. Which I'm *not* happy about. But I do it, and he slows down, then he parks us up in the garage of what I'm assuming must be their house, turns off the engine and tells me, *here we are*. I'm about to go off at him about the way he's

---

2.  In this instance, Brendan Cooper was telling nothing but the truth, even if he was guilty of exaggerating the extent of his boss' fame. After meeting and becoming friendly with the Taylors via the South Herts Chapel of Christ and the Allied Charismatics, Cooper was hired by Freddie to maintain the Fresh Meat website along with several other of Freddie's online interests, despite having no real background in IT or software engineering. It was through this professional association, Paula Deal and others have speculated, that the Coopers came to be offered a place at the Heart of Solomon – despite Brendan's somewhat meagre salary falling far short of the annual income demanded of other would-be residents.

just talked to me – remind him that this is a date, I'm not the help – but then he gets out the driver's side and opens the door for me to get out. *Holds* it open, like he's a butler and I'm the lady of the manor. And I think, maybe it's just his nerves that made him say that before, and now he feels bad about it. So, I decide to keep my mouth shut, and give him another chance.

"We go inside through the garage, into the kitchen, and they give me the tour of the house, which is... just okay. IKEA furniture, cushions from Next; all quite standard. Nothing that sets off any alarm bells. The wife says, *I'll get us a drink*, and we sit down in the kitchen while she pours us what I think is a Sauvignon Blanc, one of those brands people who don't know anything about wine think is classy. It doesn't taste great either: too bitter, no sweetness at all.

"And he asks me, do I like being a whore? Asks me exactly like that, as well. Conversational, while we're having a drink, like he's asking how long I've worked in finance.

"*Do you like being a whore, Mihaela?*

"And I'm shook. Shook, but also I'm angry, because this is *not* how clients talk to me, not if they want to *stay* clients. I go to tell him so, but as I'm talking, I start to feel... not quite right. Dizzy, sort of sleepy. *Very* sleepy, suddenly; too tired to speak or get up from the table. But my brain's still working, just, and I'm thinking, *did she put something in the wine? Did that bitch fucking roofie me?*

"But then I'm also thinking: she couldn't have, could she? Benzos don't start working straight away. It's half an hour at least before they kick in.

"Then I remember: *it was the wife who got the drinks in back at the pub...*

"And that's... the last I remember. Sitting in that

kitchen, my head spinning, him in his golf club blazer staring at me across the table and smiling. *Smiling.*

"When I came 'round again – hours later, I've found out since – I was in their bed, naked. Red marks on my wrists that'd turn into bruises, and... you know. Pain. In my thighs, my vagina. Dull pain, not sharp, but enough to make it obvious what had happened. What they'd done to me.

"The clothes I'd come in were at the bottom of the bed. Fucking folded in a pile. So, I got up and put them on – I wanted out of there, you know? – and went out into the hallway. And downstairs.

"She was in the kitchen, the wife. Fully dressed, doing the dishes by the sink. Gave me the biggest smile as I came in, like she'd been waiting for me to wake up. And she *thanked* me. Said she'd had a wonderful evening, and that they appreciated me coming all the way out to see them at home.

"I don't think I said a word the whole time she was speaking. Even when she asked if she could drop me off somewhere, give me a lift into town, I just nodded. And she did, you know – give me a lift. Drove me right to the train station, early morning with the sun still coming up, yammering on the whole way about the traffic and what she was going to cook for dinner that night in that fucking Liam Gallagher accent. I couldn't... I *didn't* take it in. Her, next to me, talking like nothing had happened... it didn't compute. Could barely hear her. Her voice was there, but far away, if you can understand that. Like listening to static drowning out the radio.

"It was shock. Obviously, it was. Dissociation – that's what my therapist thinks, anyway. Apparently, it's a stan-dard trauma response? Anyway. Between that and whatever was left in my system of what they'd used on me, I was basically a zombie for that car ride. And for the rest of that day.

"I wanted to say something, when she pulled up by the station. Even if it was just, *why?* Like: *you'd already booked me for the night, so why did you do* that?

"But she got in there first. Just as I was opening the door. And you know what she said, the *last* thing she said to me before I got out and she drove off?

"*Don't worry about the money. Brendan's already sorted it.*"

And, as McMenaman confirmed, he had – the PayPal account through which Popescu conducted sex work transactions showing receipt of a transfer of £1,600, made from Brendan Cooper's bank at 5.30am that morning.

That is: double the amount on which Popescu and the Coopers had agreed.

Like the other women in the videos – the two others currently identified, at least – Popescu declined to report the incident to police. Given her profession, the unreliability of her memory of events, the British constabulary's well-documented misogyny and hostility to sex work, and the "evidence" of the Coopers' money in her account, she believed then – as she believes now – that the odds of any charges being laid against the Coopers for the assault were virtually nil.

I'm sorry to say, I agree with her. And can't help but wonder moreover how many more victims the Coopers might have amassed in the years since her assault, were it not for their deaths and the contents of Brendan's laptop subsequently entering the public domain.

Indeed, as Phil Cooper himself observes: "what

happened to Brendan and Becky was horrific. Utterly horrific. One wouldn't wish it on anyone. But then again, seeing what Bren was capable of, what he inflicted on those poor women... One can't help but wonder if perhaps, you know... these things happen for a reason, after all."

[*Ambient cafe-style background noise: footsteps, low hum of voices, scraping of cutlery on crockery*]

**Woman:** Sorry again for running out on you before. She's fine, didn't even need stitches, but you know how it is

**Man:** Hey, don't apologise. Family comes first. I'd have been out of here like a shot if it were my wife. Those box cutters can be lethal

**Woman:** She's still convinced it was me who left them out on the side. I didn't realise we *owned* box cutters

Anyway. Shall we get on?

**Man:** Absolutely, let's

**Woman (more clearly, into recording device):** This is Gina Lewis, speaking for the second time with Phil Cooper. Date is the 22nd February 2024. Phil, would you mind confirming again that you're happy to talk to me, and you consent to this interview being used in the book we discussed?

**Man (Phil Cooper):** No problem. (clearly, into recorder) I consent, yes

**Woman (Gina Lewis):** Thanks. So: last time, we

were talking a bit about the videos, and what happened after they were leaked. Could we go back to that, if you're comfortable with it?

**PC:** (dry, mirthless laugh) I'm not sure one ought to be *comfortable* with something like that. You'd have to be a sociopath. But we can certainly go back to it

What would you like to know?

**GL:** Let's start with how you felt when you heard about them. It wasn't long after your brother's death, was it? That couldn't have been easy

**PC:** (long pause) No. No, it wasn't. (pause) Mum and dad, they were an absolute state from... the murders. Brendan dying, of course, and the circumstances, the *horror* of it, but also... There was no real body. Nothing to identify. Or... nothing *whole*. They didn't even have the closure of an autopsy, or going to see him in the morgue, or whatever the relatives usually do afterwards. The police were telling them their son was dead, then more police were telling them *how* he died, how whoever did it bloody *desecrated* him... *then* they had days and days of gutter-press people ambushing them on the way to work to try to get an inside scoop for the Sun or the Mail or whoever. From a pair of sexagenarians who'd just lost a child

(Pause)

Sofia and I went to stay with them for a bit, just to be there. It was as much for me as for them, frankly. I was driving myself mad worrying about them in that house on their own, trying to sit with their grief with the fucking paparazzi baying at the door. So, I was there when... it broke. The story

**GL:** About the laptop?

**PC:** Yes

(Pause)

I don't know that it's possible to describe what it was like for them. Finding out their son was... what Brendan was, but also, when the videos came out... *seeing* it as well, watching it play out on a screen. It was... a kind of hell, actually. Rather like that scene in A Clockwork Orange – you know the one? Where Malcolm McDowell has his eyes forced open while the Ludovico people torture him with film reels? Mum and dad, they couldn't look away. But everything they saw, every repulsive thing my brother did to those women was a knife to their hearts. You don't recover from that

(pause)

I expect you'd like to ask me what it was like for *me*, afterwards? As his brother, not just their son?

**GL:** If you want to tell me

**PC:** (pause) I want to qualify everything here with: I know I'm not the victim. Brendan died, and Becky. I can't imagine what those women in the videos suffered through. And mum and dad are still... not right, and I can't say I'm certain they ever will be. So... this isn't my story, okay? I'm very aware of that, and I don't want anything I have to say to eclipse or detract from their experiences. And I will never and *would* never defend Brendan or anything he did. I know what he was. I rather think we all do now

Perhaps, and I suppose this ties back in with what we discussed last time... a small part of me wasn't surprised by it. Because of what Brendan was like, of course. As a kid, and... later. But also... I mean, how well can one ever truly know anyone? People are capable of the strangest turnarounds, the most unanticipated actions. Look at... what's she calling herself now? *Auntie Ann?*

**GL:** (sharply) Annamaria Ainsworth – *that* Auntie Ann?

**PC:** Oh, is that what she's going by? I didn't realise. But yes, her.

**GL:** What about her?

**PC:** (slowly; half to himself) It's funny... you'd think, after all that went on at Solomon, all the trauma it brought us, I'd never want to hear the name again. But actually, I went through a real phase of devouring every scrap of info I could get my hands on about it – the place, and the people there, and the rather terrifying neo-con philosophy behind it all. A way of feeling in control of the situation, I suppose. Knowledge is power, and all that

It was all exactly as grotesque as you might imagine – although you don't *have* to imagine, I suppose, no doubt you've crawled through that particular river of shit yourself in your research. And much of it obviously I was dimly aware of already, from the American news, and from googling around when Brendan joined that church, and... (humourless laugh) doing The Handmaid's Tale for bloody A Level English. But getting on YouTube and seeing *Annie Harper* in an apron, selling herself as the Tradwife Queen and telling women to submit to their husbands by chaining themselves to the kitchen sink... well, it made me blink. Blink *hard*. Quite possibly I would have found it hilarious, had circumstances been different

**GL:** (confused) Annie Harper?

**PC:** Yes. That's her real name. Short for Annamaria, I guess? And Harper was her maiden name, presumably. Or her married name, and she's divorced since? Anyway, she was Annie Harper when she was teaching at Exeter

**GL:** Exeter *University*? She was an *academic*?

**PC:** (small chuckle) I know. It's mad, isn't it? But she was there when I was, in the Sociology department. I took one of her modules in my first year, actually – Gendered

Violence in Modern Britain. We all thought she was bloody brilliant, a proper old-school radical feminist, and not one of those TERF-y ones either. She was always very inclusive, very pragmatic. A girl I went out with in second year knew her too, from volunteering with her at a rape crisis centre off-campus. Said she was an absolute *firebrand*. You couldn't swing a cat without hitting her at a demo

So yes, I was *very* surprised to see how she'd rebranded. But then, as I say: who knows what anyone is capable of, when you get right down to it?

[*Recording ends, abruptly*]

**To**: helen.kressler@nextwavepress.co.uk

**From**: jagruti.gohil@harps.ac.uk

**Re:** Gina, Again

Hi again Helen,

I'm sorry to hound you – you probably haven't even seen the first email I sent you – but I've been reading and rereading the draft manuscript I sent you, listening over and over to that interview recording, and I really quite urgently need to hear what you think about it all. Please could you come back to me as soon as you read this, so we can discuss?

I've spoken again to the police, and – surprise, surprise – they're not taking any of this remotely seriously. I'm 90% sure they think I'm just some hysterical lesbian whose lover has left her, or that Gina's had a breakdown and is off doing an Agatha Christie in a hotel up north somewhere. But she wouldn't do that, Helen. We both know she wouldn't do that.

Whatever's happened to her, it's to do with this Auntie Ann woman, Annamaria Ainsworth. It's got to be. There's no other explanation for Gina cutting the Phil Cooper interview short the way she did in that recording. She must have heard something that set her off, something to do with that fucking Tradwife place and those horrible murders. Truthfully, Helen, I wish with every fibre of my being that you'd never commissioned her to write that book. She's a sociologist, for fuck's sake, not Bob Woodward. She's not built for this.

I know it's unprofessional, and Gina would kill me for doing it, but I might as well tell you that I've reached out to Phil Cooper myself to try to get some answers; to find out what's missing from that interview, what Gina deliberately didn't record. He was perfectly nice, exactly the sort of Bristolite eco-warrior she describes in the MS, but it was pretty much a dead end for our purposes. He confirmed what she and he talked about in their interviews, what we already KNOW they talked about, and he filled me in on what details he remembers about Ainsworth (Annie Harper, as he calls her), which he apparently passed along to Gina too, but he was as puzzled as I was by G going missing. And he seemed not to realise she'd stopped recording midway through the interview, let alone what her doing that might indicate.

Also... I've done some research of my own about Ainsworth: watched those awful videos she makes, read a few articles about her, googled her various names to see what comes up. It seems like Phil was right, and someone named Annie Harper WAS at Exeter in the early/mid 'oos, lecturing in Social Policy and Gender Studies and running an ESRC project on domestic violence. I managed to dig up a photo from an archived version of a department web site, and I can't say the physical similarity between her and Ainsworth is particularly striking, but they'd be about the same age, judging from how Harper looked in the picture, and it's not totally inconceivable that twenty years might have altered things like hair colour and face shape. Ainsworth wears a LOT of makeup, after all; she seems like she might be a dab hand at contouring, and you know how much that can change a person's appearance.

I know a couple of women at Exeter myself. Anthropologists. They've not been there long enough to have taught with Harper, but they did me a favour and asked around the various sociology and gender studies networks to see if anyone there remembered her, and what do you know? A few people did. By all accounts, Harper took voluntary redundancy in 2007, or thereabouts; one of the gender guys seems to think she was planning to move to Australia, though he didn't stay in touch with her, so he wasn't sure one way or another whether that actually happened.

Maybe I'm focusing too much on Harper. Maybe Phil Cooper has it wrong, and she and Annamaria Ainsworth are two completely different people, and Harper's living it up on the Gold Coast while Ainsworth doles out her recipes and tells girls on the internet to bow before the patriarchy. But it's a weird coincidence, isn't it? Phil thinking that in the first place?

And what about the other names Gina drops in the book – Brexit Baxter and that fascist Gorecki? They're not the sort of people who'd want a writer running around digging up dirt on them, are they? What if one of THEM found out what Gina was working on, and decided to do something about it? Okay, Gorecki's in prison, but he's got to know people on the outside, still. People who'd LOVE to go after someone like Gina if he asked them for a favour.

Then there's the really big elephant in the room: the actual murders she was writing about. Nobody was ever arrested for them, were they? They were never actually solved. So, what if Gina found out something about the murderer – who they are, even – and they had to shut her up before she took it public?

I mean, what's one more murder, when you've killed six people already and sliced up their bodies?

I'm losing my mind, Helen. I think I'm actually losing my mind.

Please reply. I don't think I can carry on like this.

Jags

**To**: jagruti.gohil@harps.ac.uk

**From**: helen.kressler@nextwavepress.co.uk

**Re:** Gina, Again

Jags,

I'm so, so sorry it's taken me this long to come back to you. I've been away in the Maldives and am only learning just now about Gina – the police left messages, but since I was out of office and where we were staying had such patchy reception, nobody thought to pass them on to me before this morning.

You haven't heard anything from her since your last email, have you?

I'm going to sit down this afternoon with the Word file you sent over, and the interview recording, and have a look at what's what. You were absolutely right about Gina not having shown me anything: she knows I trust her, and I told her she had my permission to take the story in whatever direction felt right, so she's yet to share so much as an opening paragraph with me.

Give me a few hours, and I'll come back to you. Maybe then we can catch up on the phone?

Again: I'm so very, very sorry for not replying sooner.

H.

19TH MARCH 2024, 2.31PM

**To**: jagruti.gohil@harps.ac.uk

**From**: helen.kressler@nextwavepress.co.uk

**Re:** Gina, Again

Hi Jags,

Apologies for the delay. I've been through Gina's MS and listened to the audio, and I'm sorry to say that nothing jumped out at me immediately.

Let me follow up on a couple of things and come back to you ASAP, just in case.

Don't suppose she's been in touch since yesterday?

H.

21ST MARCH 2024, 5.49PM

**To**: jagruti.gohil@harps.ac.uk

**From**: helen.kressler@nextwavepress.co.uk

**Re:** Gina, Again

Jags,

I've tugged on a few of the threads in G's MS, and actually, I think you might be right about there being something unusual there, after all.

I'd rather not go into it over email – can you let me know your number so I can give you a call?

I'm free all evening.

H.

**To**: jagruti.gohil@harps.ac.uk

**From**: helen.kressler@nextwavepress.co.uk

**Re:** Gina, Again

Still haven't heard back from you – is everything okay?

Really hoping we can speak properly soon, but in the meantime, you might want to know a few of the things I've been finding out, because they really are quite odd. Odd enough to raise questions about... the whole Heart of Solomon case, actually. Not just Gina going missing. The actual murders themselves.

Anyway. I'll tell you, and you can make up your own mind...

1. Auntie Ann/Annamaria Ainsworth IS Annie Harper – and she never moved to Australia, though she did indeed change her name when she left academia (Harper seems to be the surname of an ex-husband from decades ago).

Phil Cooper was also right about her working at a domestic violence centre while she was at Exeter. And she was on the board of a rape crisis charity in Sidmouth that's since shut down, *and* she was instrumental in getting more than a few local women rehoused after leaving abusive relationships.

So, she must have gone through some pretty radical transformations to net out at a persona like Auntie Ann. Though I'm not surprised nobody else has recognised her until now: I've seen pictures of her when she was at Exeter, and before (probably including the same one you managed to dig up), and I'd never guess it was the same woman, not in a million years.

I also had a chat, in confidence, with one of our authors (who shall remain nameless), who by extremely happy coincidence was involved with the rape crisis centre at roughly the same time as Annie Harper. She said much the same as your friend-of-a-friend: that Annie left Devon sometime 2006/7, quite abruptly, and nobody there has heard from her since.

What our unnamed author did say, though, which I thought was interesting, was that Annie was *very* jaded towards the end. Close to burnout, was how our author put it; frustrated at the limitations she had to work within, and angrier and angrier that half the service users she dealt with ended up back in abusive situations, while the actual abusers kept getting off with a slap on the wrist, if the police or the courts even intervened in the first place. It's a pretty common sentiment among people who work in gender violence prevention – I'm sure we both know that well enough, and I know Gina does – but still, it seems worth noting given the whole Auntie Ann thing.

2. You can probably file this under "weird coincidences that sometimes happen and don't mean anything," but another thing I found out – by accident, actually – when I was asking around about Annie Harper: she did her PhD at Leeds. The same place Jude Driscoll (Aisling Wilson's mum) did hers.

Again, likely just coincidence. But, and I probably should be more embarrassed than I am to admit this, I went off and played detective a bit, spoke to a couple more friends-of-friends-of-friends and disappeared down a few online rabbit holes, and... yes, it turns out Jude and Annie were postgrads at Leeds around the same time. Different departments, different subjects, and God knows they might not ever have crossed paths... though Gina's pretty clear in the MS about Jude's politics and the feminist influences on her work. So, it's maybe not a *huge* stretch to think they could have had moved in vaguely similar circles – belonged to some of the same societies and reading groups, and gone to some of the same protests. Jude doesn't mention it in her interview with Gina, but why would she? If she didn't know Annie Harper was Auntie Ann – and nobody but Phil Cooper seems to have joined the dots – then it wouldn't have been remotely salient, bringing up a woman she knew at college thirty-five years ago.

And call me paranoid, but if Jude *did* know, and she's keeping Annie's secret for whatever reason she's hardly going to mention it to Gina, is she?


3. That sweet old grandmother, Bernadette Taylor... she's keeping a secret or two of her own, and not about Freddie.

She told Gina her husband died of cancer, yes? Well, he didn't: Jim Taylor was murdered at home, in July 1983, while Bernadette and little Freddie were out at the shops. And when I say "at home," I mean the same home she's living in now with her grandkids – that bungalow where she and Gina did the interview.

The husband was stabbed – twelve times, with one of his own kitchen knives. Dorset Police had it down as a break-in gone wrong, burglars lashing out at the homeowner when they got interrupted mid-robbery. And maybe it was, but why wouldn't Bernadette have mentioned it in the interview, when she was talking about why Freddie might have developed a chip on his shoulder, and why he blamed women for everything? Finding his dad stabbed to death in the kitchen seems like the sort of thing that might've been quite formative for a boy of four.

More than that: why didn't any of the journalists who covered the Heart of Solomon case talk about it when they profiled Freddie and his family? It was forty years ago, but it made the local news, and Jim Taylor's name is right there in the archive. It's obviously not online, it doesn't show up in searches, so you have to go into the newspaper files and look for it – and you'd have to know what you were looking for to go searching in the first place – but it's there, waiting to be dug up. And get this: it was never solved, and nobody was ever charged or even arrested for it. Just like the Solomon murders.

The only explanation I can think of is that nobody, not even Paula Deal, knew there was anything there to find. That they all took Freddie, and then Bernadette, at their word when they said Jim had cancer. Freddie was the star of the show, after all. *He* was the story, not his mother.

Let's face it, *I* only went looking because of something that author I spoke to said when I told her I was doing due diligence for Gina's Solomon book. She, the author, lived all over the country in the '70s and '80s, and – without giving away any more identifying details – put in a lot of hours in a *lot* of different women's shelters. Including one in Bournemouth, *with Annie Harper*, where both of them happened to meet... you guessed it... Bernadette Taylor. And our author was *very* clear on how Jim died.

She (our author) was quite taciturn about the ins and outs of what Bernadette was doing at the shelter – confidentiality is very important to her, for obvious reasons – but it doesn't take a genius to fill in the blanks, does it?

And how does *that* fit in with the way Bernadette described her dead husband – as a gentle bloke who treated her like a queen at home?


4. It's not something I ever want to do again, but I downloaded a VPN, found the Cooper videos on a forum and watched them. All four of them.

Gina wasn't wrong; they're unbelievably disturbing. I feel sick to my stomach just thinking about them. I don't know if you've seen them – I'm going to assume you haven't, because why would any right-thinking person want to watch another human being assaulted? – but Mihaela Popescu's rape plays out much as Gina describes it. Ditto with the other two girls, Alvita Cardona Ortiz and Krystyna Adamecki.

That last girl, though – the one they never named. You can't really see her face, and there are no scars or piercings or tattoos on her, none of the sort of idiosyncrasies you might look for if you were trying to identify someone. And maybe I'm seeing things that aren't there – you're not the only one who might be losing your mind a bit over this. But there's this one shot, where Becky Cooper moves the girl ever so slightly, so you can see her for a second in profile... it's there and then it's gone, but just for that instant, she looks a *lot* like Aisling Wilson.

I'm attaching a screenshot of the shot I mean, mostly so you can tell me I'm imagining things. (Please view with caution: even static, it's not easy to look at). Logically I know it *can't* be Aisling: every man and his dog with an internet connection must have seen those videos by now. Someone would have noticed, if it was.

Unless the people who *had* to look – people like Gina, and I suppose the police – were so appalled they tried to get through it as quickly as possible, and didn't linger too long on the details, much less any single frame. And the ones who didn't *have* to watch, but who *wanted* to... didn't pay too much attention to the girl's face.

And isn't *that* a depressing thought?

Anyway. That's where I'm at.

I've had a few hypotheses rattling around my head. Some of them are vaguely plausible and some are completely outlandish; some are consistent with what Gina laid out in her MS, and some are contradictory.

I'm not sure any of them get us closer to working out where she might've gone.

But, you know... you asked me for my opinion, and to share any thoughts I might have on the MS and the audio with you. So maybe I should just go one small step further and share my thoughts on the Solomon murders as well, hastily assembled and mad though they might be.

Here goes:

**Hypothesis/Speculation A:**

### *Annie Harper was directly involved with the murders, in some capacity*

We know she had access to the Wilson house, because Jason hired her as a consultant to "teach" Aisling how to be a housewife, whatever the hell that entails. So, Harper would have known the layout of not only their property, but the Solomon estate as a whole. And presumably, nobody would have thought twice if they'd seen nice old Auntie Ann skulking about, even after she'd finished up the Wilson job.

*Why* would she have done it? Christ knows. If she really was that jaded about domestic violence and she'd decided to lean into more direct action by killing off abusive, exploitative bastards like Wilson and Cooper and Freddie Taylor... okay, I can sort of buy that. But the time and effort it would have cost her to create that Auntie Ann persona, to build up the brand in conservative circles online, all the while taking whatever steps she would have needed to stop the people who'd known her in her real life stumbling onto her by accident... that's some serious deep cover. MI6-level stuff. Is it even possible for one person to pull off something like that? We're talking about a British academic here, not Jason Bourne.

And that's before we get to her actually committing the murders herself. One small, older woman overpowering six fit, healthy adults and subduing them long enough to pull out their teeth, chop off their tongues, carve out their hearts and so on?

That feels pretty implausible to me. Even if she'd managed to drug them, if she'd slipped something (like a mega-dose of Cooper's Rohypnol) into their wine and waited for them to fall unconscious before she came out of hiding and started going wild with the pliers and the carving knives. Cutting people up like that is hard, physical work (... I imagine...). Would Harper actually have been able to do it? The flesh would surely have been pretty weak, even if the spirit were willing. I'm all for older women being powerful and capable, but there's got to be a limit.

And that's before we get to the matter of Harper disposing of six bodies on her own, in the middle of the night, so thoroughly no amount of police and amateur detectives have been able to find them *for nearly five years* – and doing it without leaving so much as a strand of her own hair on the carpet.

Unless, of course, she *wasn't* acting alone. Which brings us to...

### Hypothesis/Speculation B:
### *Jude Driscoll and Bernadette Taylor were involved too*

Don't ask me how – neither one of them comes off as much as a puppet-master in Gina's MS. But perhaps they're both better liars than I'm giving them credit for. And Gina would've been predisposed to see them as grieving mothers first and foremost, wouldn't she? She wouldn't have *wanted* to push them hard, even if she'd found any of what they told her inconsistent.

Bernadette Taylor I get, in terms of motive. Her son and daughter-in-law are monsters, she's doing most of the child-care and she doesn't want the grandsons she adores growing up poisoned by that Trad crap. Kill off Freddie and Nadine, and she's the logical choice for custody; the kids get to go home with her to Bournemouth, and they all live happily ever after.

We know she knew Annie Harper from the women's shelter all those years ago, and we can reasonably venture, given why Bernadette was probably *at* that shelter, that she's not a big fan of wife-beaters like Jason Wilson or rapists like Brendan Cooper (or Becky Cooper, for that matter, assuming she even suspected about that).

Maybe Harper sees Bernadette at Solomon while she's there with the Wilsons, the pair of them get talking... and the seeds of something are planted. A practical solution for Bernadette's problem, and a way for Annie to make happen whatever bloody vengeance on the patriarchy she's been brooding over since she left Exeter. Bernadette knows Jude Driscoll as Aisling's mum, and Annie knows her from their PhD days – and Jude *hates* Jason Wilson, and would happily see him dead along with the other misogynists who egged him on and gave him succour.

Why would Jude kill *her own daughter*, though – especially if it *was* Aisling in the video, and the Coopers raped her, too? That's the part that doesn't sit right with me. Aisling was Jude's only child, and I can't believe she was faking it completely when she was talking to Gina about her grief. She'd want to pull Aisling out of there, not let Harper and Bernadette Taylor murder her.

Wouldn't she?

That's if Aisling really *was* the girl in Jude's story; if she *was* a victim, as Jude says, and not some sort of willing accomplice to something unspeakable, the way Becky Cooper was. Or even a devil in her own right, like Nadine Taylor.

There's so much we don't know, is the problem. A world of bloody questions, and no obvious or comfortable answers anywhere.

Please come back to me on this when you can, day or

night. I really feel we should talk through some of this stuff, try to puzzle it out together. Even if 90% of what I've been thinking is absolute nonsense, there has to be *something* in it to lead us back to Gina and wherever the hell she's gone.

H.

**To**: jagruti.gohil@harps.ac.uk

**From**: helen.kressler@nextwavepress.co.uk

**Re:** Gina, Again

I'm sorry – I know I shouldn't have, but since I haven't heard back from you, or heard anything at all from Gina, I rang your office yesterday, and when they said you'd been off sick since Monday, I dug out your address from one of Gina's old submission emails and... well. You've probably figured out by now that it was me out there last night, knocking on the door. If you didn't know already.

And yes, I went around the side of the house and had a look in through the back window when nobody answered. My bad, I know. I'm sure you must have heard me shuffling the bins about, trying to get purchase; I wasn't exactly discreet about it. Annie Harper might have Jason Bourne instincts, but I don't see the Security Service calling me up for duty any time soon.

Just tell me one thing, okay? Please. For my own sanity. I'm not going to tell anyone or do anything with the information, I can promise you that. But I have to know.

Those people you were sitting with in the kitchen: were they who I think they were?

H.

FROM THE EXAMINER

16 APRIL 2024

## HUMAN REMAINS IN PEAK DISTRICT ARE TRADWIFE MURDER VICTIMS, POLICE CONFIRM

***Butchered torsos, limbs and heads found wrapped in tarpaulin on riverbank last Friday identified as Heart of Solomon corpses***

*Joey Holland, News Reporter*

The remains of five bodies washed up last week on the bank of the Peak District's River Manifold are those of five people slaughtered in 2019's 'Tradwife Massacre,' Derbyshire police said today.

Further body parts, both male and female, were recovered from the area following the initial discovery, and are understood to belong to victims ranging in age from their late 20s to their early 40s.

In a news conference this morning, officers confirmed what many online commentators have speculated since the weekend: that the remains represent five out of six casualties of the brutal slayings that took place in Nottingham's purpose-built Heart of Solomon community four years ago, for which no fully intact bodies were found at the time.

Senior Investigating Officer Detective Inspector Stefan Neath declined to identify any of the dead by name. The Tradwife victims, however, have long been known as Jason Wilson, 32; Aisling Wilson, 27; Brendan Cooper, 29; Rebecca Cooper, 26; Freddie Taylor, 40; and Nadine Taylor, 36.

All six victims were adherents of the so-called 'Trad-wife' movement, characterised by traditional conservative values and the belief that wives should "submit" to their husbands, including remaining in the home as housewives instead of going out to work.

"We're confident these are the same victims," Detective Inspector Neath said.

Police are continuing to search the twelve miles of the Manifold, which flows between Derbyshire and Stafford-shire, for further remains.

No arrests have yet been made. Detective Inspector Neath confirmed, however, that investigations into the 2019 murders, which remain unsolved, have now been formally reopened.

Members of the public with any information on either the newly discovered remains or the original murders are urged to contact Derbyshire Constabulary directly.

**To**: helenhelenhelen87@crackle.com

**From**: notginag@crackle.com

**Re:** [no subject]

Hey Helen,

I ought to start with an apology, oughtn't I? And I will: not for the vanishing act per se (more on that later), but for not calling, or coming to have all this out with you face-to-face. There's going to be a lot for you to digest in this email, I suspect – a lot for me to tell you    and I'd much rather be doing it at yours over nachos and a glass of red than through a bloody computer screen.

But we play the hand we're dealt. And the place I'm in at the moment – the place I'm in *geographically*, that is, not emotionally – doesn't offer a lot of scope for making phone calls or pouring out a Malbec. I won't go into too many details about where that is, for reasons I hope you'll understand once you've read all of this, but suffice to say, it's quite a distance from London, and the phone signal isn't great. I'm amazed I managed to find somewhere to get online, so I could send this.

(I assume you don't mind this coming through to your personal account instead of the work one, but just in case – can we keep any conversations on Cracklemail instead? No idea what Next Wave's security protocols are like, but Crackle uses end-to-end encryption... and as someone told me recently, that's quite important when you want to make sure nobody hacks into your messages. Not even the police can get into them without Crackle HQ's permission, apparently, and they're not too keen on sharing their data).

Good news first: Jags knows I'm safe. She's here with me now, actually. Pretty pissed off about me vanishing on her, and it'll be a good while before she forgives me for putting her through what she keeps telling me were the worst 2 weeks of her life... but I think she at least gets why I took off the way I did, and why I kept her in the dark about it.

She updated me on the conversations the two of you had while I was gone – and sends her own apologies for not replying to you last month. I can well imagine how strange it must have been, getting sucked into all of this out of more or less nowhere. Bet you wish you'd never said yes to commissioning the book now, eh? :)

Jags also said: she's not sure who you saw with her in the kitchen that evening you came over and knocked down the recycling bin, but she thinks they might have been a couple of Jehovah's Witnesses who caught her in a vulnerable moment and ended up staying for a cup of tea. One of them *did* look a bit like Bernadette Taylor, apparently – if that's who you thought you saw? It's an easy mistake to make; Bernadette's got a bit of a generic grandmother vibe going on, and I've seen her haircut on a *lot* of older women lately. But it wasn't her. So, I wouldn't spend any more time worrying about it.

You weren't wrong about some of the other stuff, though. Bernadette and Annie/Annamaria *did* know each other, back in the day – and they kept in touch, if you can believe it. And yes, Bernadette *did* lie to me about what happened to her husband. She's since told me: it wasn't cancer; he *was* murdered. Not that I'd bother shedding any tears for him – as I understand it (and yes, contrary to what she first told me in her interview) he was an abusive waste of skin, and, if you'll forgive the Roald Dahl reference, exactly the kind of guy you'd hope would be hit over the head with a leg of frozen lamb.

I'm not surprised you didn't find much about his murder when you went looking, by the way. Don't remember if I mentioned it in the MS you read, but Bernadette's sister June was in the police when she was alive – a WPC, as they were then. She stayed local, worked a few of the Dorset beats until she took early retirement after her breast cancer diagnosis, and I gather she and her colleagues were quite protective of Bernadette and Freddie when it all happened. They kept most of the media vultures away from them, inasmuch as they could.

I can't help you on what Annie's up to, unfortunately. She seems to have done a vanishing act of her own. Couldn't say where, though it appears she's packed up that Auntie Ann gig; last I checked, all the video channels and social media accounts had been deleted. And I do mean deleted – there's no trace of them anywhere. Maybe she finally took that trip to Australia, after all.

I assume, because I know you and you're like a dog with a bloody bone sometimes, that you're going to want me to say something about some of the other questions you raised in those last emails to Jags.

Some of them are probably better thrashed out F2F, so you might have to keep a lid on them for a while. As to those *hypotheses* you laid out, though...

Did Bernadette do it, or Annie, or Jude – or all three of them together? I have no idea. I wasn't there that night; none of us were, and even the police can't say with any real certainty how it all played out. Did they have means, motive, opportunity – that Golden Age Detective triumvirate? Sure. Bernadette was coming and going from the Heart of Solomon pretty much every day to pick up and drop off the grandkids; Annie, as you pointed out, spent a lot of time at the Wilsons' place, and might well have come across the Taylors and the Coopers while she was there. And neither Bernadette nor Annie was short of a reason to get rid of any of them, even if Annie's reasons were more... ideological than Bernadette's.

(I'm still a bit embarrassed Annie managed to pull the wool over my eyes so completely when I interviewed her that time. She missed a trick settling for academia instead of shooting for the West End).

As to whether it really was Aisling in the video, and not some other poor kid the Coopers drugged and raped in that bedroom... I suppose we'll never know, will we? It's all just guesswork. Though there *is* a resemblance there. I'll give you that.

More generally... I've thought about it a lot, these last few months – there've been times I've not been able to think of much else – and it seems to me there are a couple of likely scenarios: a couple of ways, that is, the Solomon killings could have gone.

Let me tell you, and maybe you can decide for yourself

which one seems more... plausible. I'll even steal your Hypothesis/Speculation format, to keep things orderly.

## Hypothesis/Speculation 1 (of 2):

Someone decides, for their own reasons, to rid the world of some of the worst people in it - who all happen, fortuitously, to live within a quarter mile of one another in what amounts to a closed-circuit setting. Maybe she (or he, or they) thinks she's (let's settle on that for pronouns) doing it for the right reasons – cutting the poison off at its source, even if the physical act of murder is something she finds... unpalatable. Not to mention difficult practically, if only in physical terms. You said yourself: cutting up and disposing of half a dozen bodies is no mean feat for anyone.

She weighs up her options, and concludes that she might need a bit of outside help, if she wants to put this plan of hers into action. Some of the work – the pre-work, you might call it – she can do solo, but the rest... not so much. So, she asks herself: who else can she call on? Who else has something to gain from this enterprise – or, to put it another way, who has more to gain from it than they have to lose?

And by sheer luck, it happens that she knows a couple of people who have exactly what she's looking for. People with access to the Heart of Solomon site; people who could leave and enter without anyone thinking twice; people who want the Taylors, the Wilsons and the Coopers dead as much as she does.

She reaches out to these people – maybe tentatively, maybe not. Maybe she just tells them outright what she's got in mind, and asks them if they want in on it.

However she asks them, though, they say yes. And together, they make a plan.

The night of, one of these people – on some pretext or

other – drives over to Solomon, with the others unseen in the back. Their driver parks up and, while that driver performs whatever task they're ostensibly at the place to do, the others sneak out and into the Taylors' cottage, where they find a way to hide themselves – and whatever bags of power tools and cleaning products they've brought with them to get the job done – until the right time comes.

And they wait, and they wait. Until the driver has driven away, Nadine has plated up the food she'll be serving, and the guests have arrived at the Taylors' for their weekend dinner party.

Our murderers find a way, somehow, to drug the food, or the wine: roofies are a good guess – and more than a bit ironic, given they seemed to be the Coopers' date-rape drug of choice – but I'd be inclined to go for something a bit more hardcore. Propofol or thiopental, or some other kind of anaesthetic – something you'd be absolutely certain would knock whoever ingested it out for the count. You'd hardly be worried about side effects, would you?

But then, the police never *did* find traces of any drug in what they found at the murder scene, from what I've read of the SOC and forensics reports. So, who knows what they used, these people, if they used anything. Perhaps there are drugs out there that leave no trace at all. I'm sure there are doctors or pharmacologists – or A&E nurses – who'd be able to tell you.

In any case: once the Wilsons and the Coopers and the Taylors have eaten their food and drunk their drinks... it's game on.

Why our murderers kill the *way* they kill – ripping out Freddie's heart and Nadine's teeth; serving Brendan's cock and balls on a platter and chopping off Becky's feet – is something only they know. But if I had to take a swing at it,

I'd say it's that these particular murderers probably have a deeper understanding than most of the power of symbolism and visual metaphor, of the shock factor elicited by a grisly diorama. Castrating a rapist, disfiguring a mean-girl beauty queen, amputating the hand of a wife-beater and arranging all the bits around the table for someone to find in the morning... it's like a scene from a Caravaggio, isn't it? Or The Cook, The Thief, His Wife And Her Lover. Peter Greenaway Presents... A Suburban Massacre.

At least one of our murderers, I'd say, has an artist's eye for the tableau vivant.

When they're done, they work together to transfer what's left of the bodies into bags, and they clean up the place – though maybe not too thoroughly. These are people who've been at the Heart of Solomon before, remember, and likely in the Taylors' house as well; if a SOCO in a coverall should find a stray hair or a fingerprint amongst the debris later, it would be easy enough to explain it away as something innocuous.

They take the Taylor's' car keys; drag the body-bags from the dining room to the garage, and from there into the boot of Freddie's Range Rover. Perhaps one of them is aware enough of Automatic Number Plate Recognition to switch the plates before they back out of the garage; if they are, it would explain why the car never showed up on CCTV or burned out on a country road somewhere.

And away they go. Job done.

That's one hypothesis. One way it might have happened. And what a huge bloody can of worms we'd be looking at, if any of it turned out to be true – if the murders really *did* play out that way. What a great big can of complicated, morally-ambiguous worms, guaranteed to make life even more awkward for everyone involved for years to come. I doubt even the police would want to touch an investigation like that with a bargepole, much less send it along to the CPS – if they ever had enough evidence to make an arrest, that is.

There's another option, though. A second hypothesis, if you like. One that feels a lot more straightforward, a lot more *orderly* than the first.

See what you think.


**Hypothesis/Speculation 2 (of 2):**

Freddie Taylor had a lot of enemies; for a man barely 40, he'd managed to piss off an awful lot of people before Solomon. George Gorecki and his racist minions, Simon Baxter... and that's before we get into what he might have done or said to his American backers after they'd bankrolled him. I've never met him, yet I can imagine myself hating him enough to run him through with a bread knife.

Then there's Brendan Cooper, an actual rapist who we know was also a sadistic little fuck to the people around him, and who probably wound up more than one or two of his own dealers before he got clean.

His wife, who joined in the rapes, and who stole twenty grand from her own girlfriend to finance a new cishet life in the Home Counties.

Jason Wilson, the serial abuser who even the internet thinks was capable of murder. Who knows how many women he hurt before Ingrid and Aisling; how many parents and siblings were out there baying for his blood?

So many terrible people, Helen. So many terrible people, squeezed together in one location anyone could find on a map *because Freddie showed them where it was* – and we're surprised somebody took them out?

Here's my other hypothesis. Another way the killings might have happened:

One of the wealthy, well-connected people these human monsters left in their wake gets up one morning with vengeance on his (or her, or their) mind. With his considerable resources, he hires a team of men, professionals, to make Freddie, Nadine et al pay for whatever it is they've done to him.

Make it bloody, he tells the people he's hired. Make it memorable.

*Because* these hired hands are professionals, they do their job well: starting with surveillance on the Heart of Solomon and its residents, to assess when their targets are likely to be most vulnerable. During dinner, is what they land on. When the kids are out of the way.

(They're killers, but they're not *baby* killers. Some of them are fathers themselves. Inasmuch as they draw the line anywhere, they draw it at infanticide).

*Adult* collateral, though... that's fair game. Their employer's made that clear from the get-go. Whatever other grownups are around that table with their target(s) when they go into the Taylor house to do the job... odds are, these other grownups have it coming.

Come Saturday night, our hired hands break into the house, SAS-quietly, and do what they've been paid to do. They leave a mess, as requested, and enough of a mystery to tie the police up in knots and make everyone believe there's a serial killer at work, or a sacrificial slaughter; that most of these murders are more personal than they are.

They bag up the body parts, and – using Freddie's car – they flee the scene. Maybe they'll lay low somewhere out of the country for a while once their payment's gone through. In Brazil or Mexico, or somewhere closer to home.

One of them is an animal lover. He lets the Taylors' dog out the back door as he's leaving, so the poor thing can run away to greener pastures.

They drive up north, stopping in the Peaks to dump their body-bags along the river. Not expecting, probably, that it'll be years before the bags are found.

And that's it: my second hypothesis. A lot more believable than the first, wouldn't you say? If I were the police (who are back on the case in full swing now, I suppose, since those bags washed up on the Manifold?) then I'd be much more persuaded by *this* scenario than the first one. So much easier for them to go chasing after a shadowy group of obvious villains, even if they never catch them, than whoever that other group might've been.

Bet it would play better in the papers too. "Police Seek Criminal Gang In Multiple Murder Investigation" sounds much less problematic than...

Well. You get the point.

And now... back to what *I'm* doing, I guess. And where I've been.

The short version, the version I'll be telling anyone who might have reason to ask later, is:

In the course of writing the book, I stumbled onto a couple of new interview leads that I thought might be promising and, idiot that I am, got a bit carried away and left London to pursue them. Without telling anyone, including my wife, whom I'm lucky has decided not to divorce me for my idiocy.

One of those leads was a woman, let's call her Ceri, who once knew Aisling Wilson very well, and who, after some initial reluctance, was willing to speak to me, on condition that I flew out to where she's living now. I won't tell you where – I doubt you'd know it, and I understand she's moving soon anyway – but it's pretty remote. Probably the most off-the-beaten track place I've been to, actually; hence my issues with the internet. It's lovely, though: a lot of blue sky and open space and sunsets that go on for miles. The kind of place you might dream about escaping to if you'd been trapped somewhere like Solomon. Or the Free People's Collective, come to that.

This woman, Ceri... she filled me in on a few more details about what it was like for Aisling, those last couple of years: living with Jason, surrounded by men like Brendan Cooper and Freddie Taylor. I'm not sure *unbearable* quite covers it, but it's as close a description as any.

She has some ideas of her own, of course, about what happened that Saturday night at the Taylors'. Some of what she told me – some of her *hypotheses*, you might say – were a bit far-fetched: stuff about faked deaths, counterfeit passports and planted blood that could've been ripped from a Patricia Highsmith novel. Or from one of the Reddit conspiracy theory forums that keep pointing the finger at Jason.

Some of her ideas, though... some of them, I can believe.

We had a tough time communicating initially: she's had some oral surgeries that make speaking quite difficult, so much of the conversation happened over voice-to-text. But we got there.

I can't see us getting the chance to meet again, wherever she ends up. She's a lovely woman, though. And a tough one; remarkably tough actually. You can't help but admire what she's been through to build the life she has now.

Anyway. *She* might be leaving... but I'll be sticking around here for a while, to watch some more of those sunsets. Jags too. We've got a few things to sort out back in London – the house, for one thing, and I'm not sure Jags' head of department took her seriously when she told him she was handing in her notice, so she might need to have another couple of chats with him. But we've basically decided on staying.

I'm still mulling over what I might want to do workwise, assuming we *do* stay. My appetite for writing has diminished lately, I know that much. Maybe it's the Annie Harper Effect, but I feel like doing something a bit more hands-on with my time. Something practical, socially useful. Something that actually makes a difference to women. And maybe, if I'm lucky, something that helps me exorcise some of my own demons; helps me shed some of the baggage I've been carrying around myself for however many decades.

We'll see, I suppose.

Which brings us to the book – or rather The Book, as Jags has taken to calling it. You might have twigged as much by now, but I'm not going to be finishing it – and I'm begging you with my whole heart not to release what Jags shared with you, in any form. I get there'll be renewed public interest, after what was dredged out of the river, and there'll probably be a lot of money to be made if you *do* polish it up and publish it, so this isn't something I'm asking for lightly. Christ knows I'm aware how slim your margins are at Next Wave, and how much you could do with a cash injection. But it's not a story that needs to be told – not again, and not by me. There are real people involved here, *living* people. And I don't want to fuck up their lives any more than they've been fucked up already.

You understand, right? Please tell me you understand what I'm saying to you.

I'll return the advance, of course. Return it with interest if you want me to, especially if it means we can forget you ever commissioned it, that I ever thought to bloody write it in the first place.

But to go back to where we were, when I started typing this email: I really am sorry. For the book, for the money, for the worry all of this caused you.

I hope, once you've read through all this again and maybe had time to sit with it a bit, you'll be able to forgive me. And that when I'm eventually back in London, even if it's just for a visit, we can have a proper conversation where we can both speak a bit more freely, with or without the Malbec.

Thinking of you,
    G.

# FROM DEAL WITH IT: THE PAULA DEAL PODCAST

## 27.1.2025

[Intro Music: Brass Titans - What's The Deal?]

**Paula:** Explosive stuff today, my lovelies. Ex-plo-sive stuff

(Pause)

For those of you who keep DM'ing me to let me know that you hate my *ugly bitch face* and wish you didn't have to keep listening to my *dick-wilting shriek of a voice* when you're on the tube or at the gym... good news! You'll barely hear from me *at all* today

Because today's episode – and we all know I've got a bit of an ego, so it hurts me to say this... Today's episode isn't about me. At all. For the next hour, you're going to be hearing almost exclusively from A Very Special Guest Star. So special, I'm not even going to tell you who she is. I'm going to let her tell you herself

Am I trying to build suspense here? Maybe. But I promise you, lovelies: you won't regret sticking with me

Today's episode, as my dear friend Michael Caine might put it, is going to blow the bloody doors off

I'm not *completely* cruel, and nobody likes to be kept

waiting *too* long, so I'll tell you now that this *is* a Heart of Solomon special, and it *does* relate directly to last week's news about those other Tradwife houses they're talking about building up in Stoke and Chester

Trigger warnings ahoy!

Now, just as background, in case you've been living up a tree like Chris Packham the last ten years and this is the first thing you found on your sister's iPhone – welcome back, by the way, and yes you *can* find me on Amazon and in all good bookstores, thank you for asking...

Six years ago, some very nasty people who were part of a woman-hating cult in Nottingham were murdered in some *very* nasty ways in one of their houses, and only bits and pieces of them – *bits and pieces* of them, you heard that right – were left at the crime scene. And the police, to their eternal shame, never found who did it

If you want a deep dive into the murders and the victims... guess who's *literally* written the book on them? That's right: you're listening to her. Have a look at *The New English Handmaids*, out now from Fordham & Heal. Christmas might have been and gone, but it could be the perfect birthday present for your dear old mum

So... murders. Lots of murders, blood and guts all over the place. Then *last* year, a very nice old man named Edgar Carmichael is walking his beagle up by a river in the Peak District, and what do you know? He finds a human head wrapped in plastic on the riverbank. He calls the police, and what do *they* find? More heads. And legs, and arms, and torsos. Five bodies, altogether

Five bodies police quickly identify as belonging to the people killed in Nottingham in 2019

Yes, you heard *that* right too: I said *five* bodies, not six

Three of the bodies were male, and we know now, as of

last August, who they were. Freddie Taylor, the man who set up the Heart of Solomon village, who had his heart cut out and served up on a dining plate. Brendan Cooper, the rapist whose meat-and-two-veg were lopped off with a cleaver – root and branch, my lovelies, *root and branch.* And Jason Wilson, who half of Reddit had pegged as the culprit – bet some of you lot feel silly now, eh?

The other two were female. Nadine Taylor, Freddie's American wife, who got a scalping and her teeth pulled out by their caps – and Becky Cooper, the *other* rapist. Myra Hindley to Brendan's Ian Brady

But who was missing, you ask?

That would be Aisling: Aisling Wilson, Jason's long-suffering missus

You can read all about Aisling and her background in *The New English Handmaids*, if you're so inclined. But what you need to know *right now* is: despite the lack of a body, we all still very much thought she was dead. The woman's *tongue* had been cut off and left at the scene; there were *buckets* of her blood soaked into the carpet! Not to mention that *her husband and four of her friends had all definitely been killed*

Aisling's body hadn't washed up on the riverbank like the others. But it would, we told ourselves. It was just a matter of time

We were wrong though, my lovelies. Because today, in this very episode, I can reveal that Aisling Wilson is not only alive, but has *reached out to me directly* with a pre-recorded interview

And my word, does she have a story to tell

Now, before any of my legal-eagle listeners start sweating about any repercussions, etc. – let me reassure you that I've run it past my solicitor already, who's had a good listen to the mp3 file I was sent, and we'll be passing it, and the anonymous email that came with it, along to the relevant authorities shortly, as soon as we've wrapped up here

As I said at the beginning: it's explosive stuff, and I want all of you to hear it first

I've played it beginning to end about five times now, every time with my jaw on the floor, and there's *so much* I want to say about it, lovelies. So. Much

But before I do... well, I think it's only fair you hear it for yourselves, don't you?

So, without any further ado... here's Aisling

(Pause)

[Recording plays]

**Interviewer (female, unidentified):** Let's start with your name. Would you mind repeating it for me?

**Faintly robotic female voice:** Aisling Driscoll. Formerly Aisling Wilson. Though I don't go by either of those names now

**Interviewer:** Just to be clear: you're talking to me today via text-to-speech software? This isn't your real voice that anyone who might be listening is hearing?

**Aisling:** No. I mean, yes. I'm using voice software. So, sorry if there's a delay when we're talking, it takes a minute for me to type out replies

**Interviewer:** And can you explain *why* you're using it?

**Aisling:** I can, yeah. I'm using it because I have trouble being understood when I try to speak. I don't have a tongue, so it's hard to form a lot of the sounds

**Interviewer:** You don't have a tongue?

**Aisling:** No. I cut it out six years ago, after I killed my husband

(Pause)

**Interviewer:** Right. Well. That was... definitive. (Pause) Could you elaborate on that? Obviously, the point of this interview is to... explain a bit about what happened that night at the Heart of Solomon, from your perspective. So where would be a good place for us to start?

**Aisling:** Up to you. Do you want to start with the murders, or in the run up to them? Presumably Paula will want to know what made me do it. I listen to her podcast, and I've read her books. She likes a clear motive

**Interviewer:** The run-up, then. Maybe you can tell me a bit about your marriage to Jason and your time at Solomon? Or your experience with Brendan and Becky Cooper, if you feel comfortable reliving it?

That'll probably make it easier for everyone to understand your motivations. We can cover the logistics later

**Aisling:** The logistics?

**Interviewer:** How you did it. (Pause) How you killed Jason. And the others

**Aisling:** Right. (Pause) Well, the world and his wife seem to know Jay wasn't... the greatest husband, so I don't know if it's worth me dwelling on that. Everything my mum's told you already is basically true. He was controlling, he hit me, he didn't like me doing anything without his say-so, he stopped me seeing people when he wasn't there. It's the same story you hear thousands of women tell. The same one his exes told that documentary guy, Alex O'Neill. People are probably sick of hearing it, the amount it gets in the news that some girl in Liverpool was strangled or a woman my mum's age in Brighton snaps one morning and stabs the man who's been beating her up for thirty years

But the familiarity of it, how often it happens... that doesn't make it any easier to live through when you're *in* it

(Pause)

Jay was always bad. You always had to monitor his moods, keep an eye on which way the wind was blowing for him so you knew when he needed placating, or when the best you could do was try to stay out of his way. But he got a lot, lot worse when we were in at Solomon. I think before he'd felt he had to keep the abuse under wraps, that people wouldn't think it was acceptable to punish your partner by slapping her or making her stand in the corner until she'd learned her lesson. But once we'd moved it was par for the course

Freddie and Nadine were big on Christian domestic discipline – do you know it? It's exactly what it sounds like. They encouraged all the husbands to practice it on their wives if they talked out of turn

Jay loved that. It was like Christmas for someone like him

That was how I ended up with Brendan and Becky in that bedroom. As punishment

Jay knew all about them. What they were into, what they did to the girls they brought home. Brendan used to brag about it when he came over to watch the football. You've seen Jay, what a big guy he was, how built, but Brendan was quite skinny, a bit androgynous-looking, and I think it made him feel more of a man to talk to someone like Jay about the women he'd fucked. What he'd give them to make sure they stayed quiet while he was fucking them

Freddie and Nadine didn't know about that. They wouldn't have liked it if they'd known. Both of them were quite proper. Not just conservative or religious because it suited them, like Jay and Brendan and a lot of the other guys at Solomon. No, they really believed in all that stuff about traditional marriage and family and the man being the head of the household. And they wouldn't have stood for it if they'd known what Brendan was into. They'd have kicked him and Becky to the curb

But Jay always let Brendan brag about it. Even egged him on a bit sometimes. It was horrible to hear the way he talked about those girls, I hated having to hear it, but Jay would never let me leave the room when Brendan was over. He'd always make me stay and listen. It was a power thing, I think. And a way of showing off to Brendan the way Brendan showed off to him. Like: look how well I've got her trained. She doesn't even move unless I tell her to

The horribleness was always at a distance though. Something I knew about second-hand, not something that actually affected me directly. Then Jay and I had a row, and I lost my temper and talked back to him when I shouldn't have, and he decided I needed to be taught a lesson. So, he gave me to Brendan

I'm not going much into what played out then. You've seen the videos, you know how Brendan and Becky liked to operate. Jay didn't tell me exactly what was going to happen, but he didn't have to. I'd heard Brendan talk about it often enough. Jay made me have a shower, stood in the bathroom and watched me, then told me we were going next door, no arguments. And I'd see what happened to bitches who didn't do what they were told

I didn't say no. I'm not going to pretend otherwise, it's too late for that. He took me there, they gave me a glass of wine to drink that knocked me out, and when I woke up I was in their bed, bleeding. And it was obvious what Brendan had done. How Jay had punished me

We didn't talk about it after. I got dressed and walked

home and got back in the shower, then into bed next to Jay, and that was it. Done. All Jay said was: you'll listen to me now, won't you? And that was all he ever said

(Pause)

**Interviewer:** I'm so sorry

**Aisling:** No need. It's done. All done now

(Pause)

**Interviewer:** These ideas about discipline Jason had – were they why he reached out to Auntie Ann for advice? To help keep you in line?

**Aisling:** Jay didn't find Annie. She messaged us

**Interviewer (surprised):** Oh. I didn't realise that

**Aisling:** Why would you? (Pause) I hadn't even heard of her before she got in touch. Jay didn't like me being on my phone

She sent him a DM on Instagram, saying she'd been following Nadine and the Solomon developments, and wanted to introduce herself and the services she offered, in case any of us were interested

**Interviewer:** Services? Could you say a bit about what they were?

**Aisling:** Cookery lessons. Household budgeting. Cleaning, ironing. All the things a good wife is supposed to do for her husband

And the weirder things. Behaviour modification. How to take discipline. Obedience lessons, basically. Training you to be a better wife, the way you'd train a dog

That was what she told Jay. She said the Tradwife stuff was something she'd been doing as a hobby, since she retired. But that she did a bit of consultancy on the side for men like him, traditional husbands, because she found it satisfying. She told him she didn't have a lot of clients, and they were quite a select list, mostly families in the States who'd had her flown over there, but she'd read about what Freddie and Nadine were doing with Solomon and she loved the idea, so wanted to do what she could to help. Even if she had to do it at a discount

**Interviewer:** And Jason was keen?

**Aisling:** Oh, yeah. He liked that he thought he'd be getting a discount, that he could have something only rich Americans usually had, but at a bargain rate. And he was making money hand over fist by then. We could more than afford it

But really what he loved was the idea of someone breaking me in and making me more compliant. Guess he didn't think he'd broken me enough already

And she was sort of famous, remember. Internet famous. Everyone in the community knew of her, from her Instagram and her videos

**Interviewer:** The community?

**Aisling:** Other Tradwives and their husbands. People like us

(Pause)

**Interviewer:** So, he said yes to the offer? He invited Auntie Ann to stay with you?

**Aisling:** For a fortnight. He paid her ten grand, cash, which she said was about half her usual fee for two weeks' work, and then he got me to make up the spare room for her. A week later, he picked her up from the train station, and there she was. Living with us

(Pause)

You met Annie last year, didn't you? When she was still doing the Auntie Ann thing. So, you know how she came across when she was putting it on. Like Hyacinth Bucket, crossed with a really strict headmistress. She scared the absolute shit out of me when she first walked in

**Interviewer:** And what happened then, after she arrived?

**Aisling:** First thing? Exactly what she'd promised Jay. Introduced herself, then set her bags down, put her apron on and dragged me off into the kitchen to show me how to roll out dough. I thought the whole fortnight was going to be like that: cooking lessons and etiquette lessons and sermons about how to please your man

Then Jay left to go to the pub, and everything got a bit more interesting

**Interviewer:** What does that mean?

**Aisling:** She dropped the act. Right away, more or less. It was incredible to watch the change in her. In her face, the way she spoke, even her body language. Like that scene with Verbal Kint in the Usual Suspects: one minute he's limping away, the next he's straightening up and getting into a limo and you realise you've been Keyser Soze'd. Annie walked in like Doris Day's grandma, but as soon as Jay went out, I could've been taking to Germaine Greer. Or that radical feminist woman who shot Andy Warhol. Valerie Solanas

(Pause)

"Your mum sent me." That was what she said. That her and my mum were friends, and my mum had asked her to come and help me get out of Solomon. Get me away from Jay

I actually thought there might be something wrong with her when she said that, that maybe she wasn't quite right in the head. How would someone like *her* know my mum? My mum, who insisted on me listening to Joan Baez and Joni Mitchell from the day I was born? Who keeps a portrait of Frida fucking Kahlo in her sitting room?

But then she started talking. About how they'd met at

uni, and been friends ever since even though Annie was a bit older, and how mum had been talking to her about me and my situation with Jay, and had asked her to help. That was what she called it, by the way: *your situation*

I wouldn't have believed her. Why would anyone believe that? But she knew stuff, about mum. Stuff you wouldn't know unless you knew her really well. I won't say what it was, there's no need, but she absolutely wouldn't have been able to tell me it if her and mum hadn't been close. And I already knew how worried mum was about me, living with Jay. She'd have tried to come and get me to take me home herself if there'd been a chance of Jay letting her through the door. So, the more I heard, the more plausible it started to sound

**Interviewer:** You didn't find it strange, that someone purporting to be... what would you call her, a Tradwife-trainer? That someone like that would be friends with your mother? And that your mother would trust her enough to send her after you?

**Aisling:** Of course I found it strange. But she explained that, too. Told me the whole backstory of the Auntie Ann thing, the character she'd invented

**Interviewer:** Could you expand a bit on that - *the Auntie Ann thing?*

(Pause)

**Aisling:** What she told me, and what I assume she'll tell the world if the police ever catch up with her, is that she'd set it all up as a sort of cover story. The videos, the social media accounts, even the way she dressed and carried herself and the work she'd had done on her face. It was all part of an act. A new identity she'd made up for herself, so she could do what she needed to do

**Interviewer:** Which was?

**Aisling:** Rescuing people. People like me, who'd got themselves into *situations* they couldn't get out of

**Interviewer:** Other women in abusive relationships?

(Pause)

**Aisling:** Something like that, yeah. (Pause) Being Auntie Ann... it got her into places she wouldn't have been let into otherwise. Into people's homes, their private spaces. And she didn't even need to ask to be let in, because when they thought she was like them, that she was on the same page as them, men like Jay just... invited her in. They wanted her there, keeping an eye on their wives

It was sort of perfect, to be honest. Very Mission Impossible, probably not something you'd believe if you read it, but perfect. Annie's a smart woman

**Interviewer:** And what did she suggest, in terms of getting you away from Jason? What was the plan of action she proposed?

(Pause)

**Aisling:** That we kill him. And Freddie and Nadine, for setting up Solomon and making it *a femicidal Petri dish* – her words again. She wanted to make a statement. And she wanted to help out my mum. So: two birds, one stone

**Interviewer:** It didn't strike you as an extreme solution? There had to have been other ways she could have got you away from Jason

**Aisling:** He would have found me. He used to tell me that all the time: *try to leave me, and I'll find you, and once I'm finished with you, you'll be sorry you ever tried.* I believed it, too. I still believe it. He wasn't someone who'd just let you leave

**Interviewer:** I see

**Aisling:** I know you do. Though whether anyone else

will remains to be seen, I suppose. (Pause). And that was it. The run-up to it

**Interviewer:** To the murders?

**Aisling:** Yes. (Pause). Annie stayed with us for two weeks altogether. Jay was out for most of that. So, we had a lot of time to plan

(Pause)

**Interviewer:** You didn't mention the Coopers just now. I understand your motivation for wanting to be free of Jason, and your mother's, and I can sort of understand where Annie was coming from on Freddie and Nadine, if she really did want to make a statement about Solomon. But why Brendan and Becky?

**Aisling:** Do you really have to ask?

(Pause)

**Interviewer:** It was your idea, to kill them too?

**Aisling:** Not my idea. My *condition*, for going ahead with it. If we were going to do it, I wanted to make sure we did it properly. That we got rid of them as well

**Interviewer:** People are going to be listening to this recording when we're finished, probably a lot of people. You aren't worried about coming off as... perhaps a little unsympathetic?

**Aisling:** I slit my husband's throat with a machete. I cut off Brendan's balls with a bread knife while he was still alive to watch me do it. I think we're a bit past trying to garner public sympathy

**Interviewer:** Fair enough. (Pause). Talk me through the plan you made with Annie

**Aisling:** We decided the easiest thing was to do it over dinner, so we'd have everyone together in the same room. I wanted to do it at ours, but Annie was adamant it had to be at Freddie and Nadine's, for the look of things. So, a couple of days before she was due to leave, she told Jay she thought it might be nice if I cooked something for a few of the neighbours, to show off what I'd learned from her. How much I'd improved in the kitchen since he'd hired her

I don't know if she nudged Jay into landing on Freddie and Nadine and Becky and Brendan, or if he came up with them himself. But it was definitely her who told him we should do it at Freddie and Nadine's. She told him: they're the linchpins of the community, which means they're the ones you want to impress. And Jay was all about impressing people, so he went for it right away. Nadine was probably just happy she wouldn't have to do all the cooking herself

You know how it went from there. We settled on a date for me to do the dinner, two weeks after Annie had left so it wouldn't look too suspicious when the police came to investigate later. And when the date came, I went over to Freddie and Nadine's with a load of ingredients for cooking, a boxful of tools Annie told Jay were essential for carving up the meat, and half a dozen syringes full of drugs to unload into the wine, so everybody was nice and pliable when we needed them to be

**Interviewer:** What sort of drugs were these? There was no mention of any drug in the medical examiner's report at the time

**Aisling:** No idea. They came from one of Annie's friends, a woman who used to be a nurse. I'm not sure even Annie knew the exact mixture. Just the effects she was after

**Interviewer:** Which were?

**Aisling:** Compliance, but without any loss of consciousness. So, they'd be awake while it was happening. She wanted them to know what we were doing to them as we were doing it

**Interviewer:** (Quietly) And who was she, the nurse who provided these drugs?

**Aisling:** I couldn't tell you. Sorry. Annie knows people all over the world. It could've been anyone

(Pause)

**Interviewer:** What *did* happen, that night?

**Aisling:** I made the dinner. Nadine was hovering around the kitchen, pretending she was supervising, but she was on her phone checking her Instagram practically the whole time, so it wasn't like there was a lot of subterfuge involved on my part

She served it, of course, because she had to be involved somewhere. She even poured the wine, which made me laugh. Then they toasted Jay for masterminding the meal, downed their wine... and a couple of minutes later, they were flopping around the table like a school of fish. Couldn't speak, couldn't stand up. Jay actually fell onto the floor trying to get up off his chair. He landed on his arm. I heard it break

**Interviewer:** And what then?

**Aisling:** Then I let mum and Annie in, and we got to work

**Interviewer:** Your mother was there?

**Aisling:** Yes. She's given me permission to tell you, so don't worry about dropping her in it. She wants people to know she was involved

**Interviewer:** We'll circle back to that one, I think

**Aisling:** We probably should. But yes: I can confirm she was at Freddie and Nadine's that night

(Pause)

Annie had told me in broad strokes what they'd do: how they'd get into Solomon earlier in the day, then find a way into the house ahead of everyone arriving for dinner. They'd been waiting there hours before I gave them the shout, in the utility room. Nadine talked a good game about being a housewife, but we all knew nobody but the cleaner ever went in there

**Interviewer:** And then, just to be absolutely clear: the three of you killed them? The Taylors, the Coopers and your husband?

**Aisling:** Yes. Do you want the details?

**Interviewer:** No. No, I think whoever ends up listening to this should be able to... connect the dots. (Pause) I assume the gruesomeness of the scene you left behind was Annie's way of making her statement?

**Aisling:** Partly. Though I was quite in favour of making a statement of my own by then. Especially about Brendan and Becky

And we needed them to bleed. It was really important that they lost a lot of blood, so it was clear to everyone they actually were dead, and not just missing

**Interviewer:** And that *you* were, too

**Aisling:** Yes. Annie had been drawing blood from me every day she was with us, to store and chuck onto the carpet of that dining room later. She knew what she was doing

**Interviewer:** And is that why you cut out your tongue? As proof of your own death?

**Aisling:** Yeah. We'd talked about going with a hand, something that would be less life-altering, but it didn't seem radical enough. You can lose a hand and live, but who in their right mind would cut out their own tongue as misdi-rection? It had to look real

**Interviewer:** Did it hurt?

**Aisling:** Like you wouldn't believe. Annie tried to be gentle, and she cauterised it right away, but there's really only so much you can do it to minimise pain with an injury like that. I blacked out for a few minutes

**Interviewer:** And then?

**Aisling:** Then we threw the bodies in the boot of Freddie's Range Rover, put Augustus in the back with mum… and left. He was a lovely dog. He deserved better than Freddie and Nadine as owners, and Annie knew a couple who'd agreed to take him in. So, he came with us

**Interviewer:** Why not leave the bodies where they were?

**Aisling:** You're too clever to be asking that question. How would it have looked, if there'd been five bodies at the house, not six, and mine was the only one missing? We had to get rid of them

Annie had a new passport ready for me, so I could get out of the country once I'd healed up a bit. Though we knew she was intending to stay where she was for a while. She has a house in the Peaks. *Had* a house in the Peaks. And she wanted to keep the Auntie Ann thing going as long as she could, so she could reach out to other women like me if she needed to. And to cover her own arse, presumably. Nobody asked where she'd disappeared to, that nice old lady who'd been staying with the Wilsons just before they pegged it

She dropped us off near Gatwick, at an Airbnb she'd rented for us. She never told us what she was going to do with the bodies, though we know now, don't we?

**Interviewer:** Do you think she knew they'd wash up eventually when she dumped them in that river?

**Aisling:** I'm sure she did. She probably thought they'd show up sooner. It isn't the Mekong Delta, is it?

**Interviewer:** And where is Annie now?

**Aisling:** You know I'm not going to tell you that.

Though don't worry, whoever's listening to this: wherever she is, I'm sure she's doing the Lord's work

(Pause)

**Interviewer:** Okay. Let's cut to the chase, then. Why are you telling me this now, like this? Why are we doing this interview? I'm sure people listening will wonder what you stand to gain by confessing to mass murder in front of an audience of millions

**Aisling:** Because they want to do it again. They want to make Solomon again. And I'm not going to let that happen

**Interviewer:** Who is *they?*

**Aisling:** The Hobart Trust. The American nutjobs who funded Freddie. They want to open up more sites like Solomon, in the UK and the States, now a few years have passed since the murders and all the bad publicity that came with them. They've bought the land already. We can't afford to let them go any further down the line

**Interviewer:** There's been nothing about this in the press. British *or* American

**Aisling:** No. But Annie and her friends have their ears to the ground. They've read the project plan, all five hundred and fifty pages of it. It's happening. You just haven't heard about it yet

(Pause)

**Interviewer:** And how does you confessing to the murders put a dent in these plans?

(A brittle, abrasive rattling that might be laughter. The laughter of someone with no tongue)

**Aisling:** Because this isn't a confession, as well you know. This is a threat

I'm still out here. My mum's still out here. And more importantly: Annie and her friends are still out here.

Nobody's caught us. Nobody's *going* to catch us. And if they do, so what? We're not afraid of prison. It's not going to be worse than living with Jay, is it?

I'm speaking to the Hobart Trust directly now, when I say this. And to anyone thinking of working with them, or thinking it might be a good idea to move into one of their villages so they can treat their wives and all the other women in their lives like it's 1664

We've killed before. And we'll kill again if those communities are built. Places like Solomon shouldn't exist in the world. And people, men like Freddie and Brendan and Jay... they need to know that if they build those places, then we'll find them. And we'll do what we did at Solomon all over again, and worse

You'll never be safe. We'll make sure of it

**DantesInferno:** Has anyone listened to that Paula Deal cunt's podcast from yesterday yet? It's mental

**ArnoldPress04:** yeah i heard it. total shit. like 2 old women and a little bitch like aisling are gonna be able to do that. they'd break a hip

**WarioWaster11** whats this?

**DantesInferno:** Heart of Solomon case mate. Jason Wilson's wife confessed to doing them all in with her mum and some other lady

**ArnoldPress04:** but like i said its not true

**WarioWaster11** I thought she was dead?

**DantesInferno:** they never found her body with the others. Looks like she's still alive

**ArnoldPress04:** bollocks is she. it wasnt even her real voice on the recording, just a text-to-speech. sounded like stephen hawking

**TheBeekeeper:** yeah, i heard it. they didn't even use AI for the voice. like they couldn't even be bothered to pretend it was really her

**DantesInferno:** Who was it, then? @TheBeekeeper

**TheBeekeeper:** how do I know? could be anyone. could be deal trying to boost her shit ratings with a fake news story

**PsychoKillerKeskaSay:** Sounded convincing to me. And if it's true, then Wilson needs getting. All of them need getting

**ArnoldPress04:** its not true brother, don't sweat it @PsychoKillerKeskaSay

**DantesInferno:** @ArnoldPress04: What about all the stuff she said, then? About new Tradwife houses opening up?

**FuckYouIWontDoWhatYouTellMe:** I'd be into that if they are

**TheBeekeeper:** @FuckYouIWontDoWhatYouTellMe no you wouldnt, because its all MADE UP BULLSHIT

**ArnoldPress04:** yeah. you really think theres some fucking Old Lady Mafia out there plotting more mass murders?

**TheBeekeeper:** @DantesInferno you've been watching too much Ocean's 8 mate

**DantesInferno:** Fuck off

**JamesGiantPeach:** wouldn't it be sort of awesome if there were though? Like, a full-on army of murdering grannies, and they kept getting away with murder because nobody believed they could properly do it?

**ArnoldPress04:** whatever gets you off mate @JamesGiantPeach

**TheBeekeeper:** make sure you wear a wrist support @JamesGiantPeach

**ArnoldPress04:** lol

**FuckYouIWontDoWhatYouTellMe:** lololol

**Jason_Statham101:** #crypto is changing the game. Is your wallet ready? Profit like I did with UpsideDown-Coin. Thank you **@BitcoinMasterJ**!

**ELECTRA SCOOPS TRADWIFE MURDERS REIMAGINING**

**Grace McCluskey** at Electra has snapped up **Paula Deal** and **Gina Lewis**' *Aisling's Story*, "a fictional *Wide Sargasso Sea*-like recreation" of the still-unsolved Heart of Solomon killings, in a seven-figure pre-empt.

Journalist Deal is the author of *The Keeper of Wives* and *The New English Handmaids*, both of which explored the Heart of Solomon case from a more conventional true-crime perspective. Former sociologist Lewis is the writer of 2022's bestselling *The Eight Half-Lives of Cleo McAllister*.

Deal made waves this January following the broadcast on her *Deal With It* podcast of an apparent "confession" from still-missing Solomon victim Aisling Wilson – a confession since widely debunked as a PR hoax intended to generate interest for her (at the time undisclosed) collaboration with Lewis.

Terms were negotiated by **Helen Kressler** of Samsara Literary, formerly of Next Wave Press. Lewis, Kressler has said, intends to donate her half of any shared royalties to Together We Stand, a survivors' charity founded this year by Bernadette Taylor, whose son Freddie died at the Solomon massacre. Both Taylor and Aisling's mother Jude Driscoll have publicly supported the decision to publish *Aisling's Story*, despite the controversy surrounding its content.

No publication date has been announced.

# ACKNOWLEDGMENTS

Publishing anything is a team effort. My thanks and endless gratitude, therefore, to the many people who've helped bring Tradwife out into the world, including but by no means limited to:

My editor, Andy Spencer - still the best in the business;

Ruth Anna Evans, for her incredible cover design;

Mrs Williams, the most capable woman I know, whose judgement I value above pretty much everyone else's;

The wonderful Sharron Elwell and Kev Harrison (... you beautiful hedgehog of a man, you...), for their kind words and boundless support;

The Indie Horror Chapter, a constant source of encouragement for everyone involved - with particular shoutouts to Leigh Kenny, Graeme Reynolds, Matty-Bob Cash, Dave Watkins, MJ Mars, Sarah Jules, Elizabeth J Brown, the mighty Chris Jones... and Trish Wilson, who somehow manages to keep the stray cats herded and the whole thing upright;

My parents, who will probably never read this but to whom I'm very grateful anyway;

And my partner, Shauna Mc Eleney - the Nefarious Bat-in-chief, without whom I'd be utterly lost.

See you all next time...

# ABOUT TC PARKER

TC Parker is a writer and researcher based in Leicestershire, where she lives with her partner and family.

The author of the El Gardener crime trilogy (*The Debt, The Push* and *The Remembrance*, recently reissued as *The Long Con* omnibus) and the horror novels *Saltblood, A Press of Feathers, Salvation Spring, Hummingbird* and the *Hummingbird Murder Mysteries*, she's been a copywriter, a lecturer and, very briefly, an academic. Now she runs a semiotics and cultural insight agency by day and dreams up stories at night, when the kids are asleep.

Visit her online at www.tcparkerwrites.com

# ALSO BY T C PARKER

Saltblood

Salvation Spring

A Press of Feathers

Hummingbird

To Coventry: A Hummingbird Murder Mystery

Consequential: A Hummingbird Murder Mystery

The Long Con: An El Gardener Omnibus

The Debt

The Push

The Remembrance

Taking Flight: A Sapphic Screwball Comedy

## ABOUT NEFARIOUS BAT PRESS

Nefarious Bat Press is a female-owned independent publisher specialising in queer horror, crime and dark fiction.

Find them online at www.nefariousbatpress.com

# THE DEBT

## EL GARDENER BOOK 1

**WHO DO YOU TRUST, WHEN EVERYBODY LIES?**

El Gardener is used to telling lies – as a con-artist, she's made a career of it.

But when she takes on what seems to be a routine job as a favour to the woman who trained her, she finds herself plunged into the most personal con of her career – taking down the man who killed her mother 20 years before.

Joining forces with a team of talented but enigmatic con-women, all with their own reasons for wanting payback, El plots his downfall. But it isn't long before she's questioning their motivations, the secrets they're keeping... and what she thinks she knows about her past.

How much is she willing to gamble for revenge? And how far can she trust the women she's thrown in with?

*Who **do** you trust, when everybody lies?*

# HUMMINGBIRD

**THERE'S A STORM BREWING IN GALLOW: ANGRY PARENTS, PROTESTS AT THE SCHOOL, A NEW PRIEST UP AT THE CHURCH WITH SOME VERY CLEAR IDEAS ON SIN... AND AN UNFAMILIAR FACE IN THE COTTAGE ON THE EDGES OF THE VILLAGE, CARVING SCULPTURES OUT OF SKIN AND BONE.**

**IT'S A POWDER KEG. EVEN BEFORE THE PROTESTORS START DISAPPEARING...**

Jodie doesn't want trouble - just to be left alone to raise her son in peace.

Tanya wants more God and less wickedness in her own son's studies.

Tara wants to leave her complicated past behind her, if only it would let her go.

And all Jonas wants is to get some work done - and if he can make peace with his father while he's at it, then so much the better.

But the woman in the cottage and the priest up at the church - they have very different goals in mind. And Jodie and Tanya, Tara and Jonas... they're about to get caught in the crossfire.

**With a Foreword by Stephanie Ellis, author of PAUSED and THE FIVE TURNS OF THE WHEEL**

*"Hummingbird is the kind of novel labyrinth where the unexpected lurks around every corner. Parker's mosaic holds layer upon layer of gripping characters and supernatural tricks in a Pulp Fiction-esque horror show, where a monster's only weakness is another kind of monster. Immediately engrossing."* -- **Hailey Piper, Bram Stoker-Award winning author of QUEEN OF TEETH and THE WORM AND HIS KINGS**